SCARY SCHOOL
THE NORTHERN FRIGHTS

SCARY SCHOOL
THE NORTHERN FRIGHTS

By
DEREK THE GHOST

Scary pictures by
SCOTT M. FISCHER

HARPER
An Imprint of HarperCollinsPublishers

Library of Congress Cataloging-in-Publication Data
Kent, Derek Taylor.
    The northern frights / by Derek the Ghost ; scary pictures by
Scott M. Fischer. — 1st ed.
        p.   cm. — (Scary School ; #3)
    Summary: Charles Nukid and his friends are chosen to be
exchange students at Scary School's terrifying counterpart, Scream
Academy, where they encounter polter-bears, abominable snowmen,
trolls, and the dreaded Ice Dragon.
    ISBN 978-0-06-196098-7 (hardcover bdg.)
    [1. Supernatural—Fiction.   2. Schools—Fiction.
3. Prophecies—Fiction.   4. Humorous stories.]   I. Fischer, Scott M.,
ill.   II. Title.
PZ7.K4132Nor   2013   2012022160
[Fic]—dc23   CIP
                                                              AC

Typography by Erin Fitzsimmons
13 14 15 16 17   LP/RRDH   10 9 8 7 6 5 4 3 2 1
❖
First Edition

To my family
(both *living* and ghosts)—
Bingo, Mom, Dad,
the Emersons, the Rosses,
and my grandparents

Contents

Caveat
discipulus

Re~ reintroduction

Hello, brave readers! It is I, your humble narrator, Derek the Ghost. You know, the kid who kicked the bucket when a science experiment went terribly wrong in Mr. Acidbath's class. It was no biggie. I turned into a ghost and still had to go to school the next day.

Thank you for joining me on your third visit to Scary School. Because you've been so loyal, I think it's safe to say that we're good friends now. And if you're reading this book without having read the first two,

I'm sure we'll be buddies by the time you're finished.

I know I usually start these introductions with something fun and silly. But now, there's simply no time for that. You see, a group of Scary School students was chosen to spend a week at Scream Academy—the scariest scary school in the world. Rather than hang out at Scary School, I decided to follow them and see what it was like there. Let me tell you, not even *I* was ready for how terrifying it was!

And when an eleven-year-old ghost like me gets scared out of his wits, you know you're in for some spectacular frights.

Normally, I would wish you good luck in surviving your time at Scary School, but this time, I think the poor Scary School students who were chosen to visit Scream Academy could use it more, so why don't you join me in wishing them good luck?

Ready? One . . . two . . . three. . . . Good luck!

1

Vacation Is Over

Petunia walked into Dungeon 5B five minutes before class started on the first day of school after winter break. She breathed a sigh of relief that the rest of her sixth-grade classmates were already in their seats. On the first day of school after summer break, her classroom had been empty, which led to a very scary rescue in Jacqueline's haunted house. She had no desire to go back there.

Frank (which is pronounced "Rachel") was fixing her brown, frizzy hair when Petunia entered. Frank jumped up out of her seat to hug her but recoiled when she saw that Petunia's long purple hair was once again swarming with bees. So they high-fived from a safe distance.

"Hi, Petunia! I missed you so much! Did you get any good presents for the holidays?"

"Just some new books," Petunia replied.

"I got a new jump rope that has an automatic counter. I got up to sixteen million jumps by New Year's Eve. Using Monster Math that's like—"

"Fifty-five trillion jumps," a voice answered.

Petunia and Frank turned around to see a girl wearing all black.

"Oh, hey," said Petunia. "You must be new. I'm Petunia. What's your name?"

"My name is swiftness. My name is stealth. I will know these like I know my name," the girl in black replied in a deadly serious tone.

Petunia and Frank looked at each other and shrugged.

"Oookay," said Frank. "How do you know Monster Math?"

"My master was the greatest monster mathematician who ever lived. An evil dragon the size of a mountain took him from me. Have you seen this dragon?"

Petunia and Frank looked at each other again.

"Umm . . . no," they replied.

The girl in black squinted her eyes. Then she asked, "Is this the class of the one called King Khufu?"

Petunia replied, "No, that's the other sixth-grade class."

In a blink, the girl in black vanished. Don't worry; there will be much more about her very soon.

As Petunia took her seat, she looked around the room. As usual, Penny Possum was sitting in the back corner, trying to go unnoticed. Fritz was wearing his swim goggles and swim trunks, hoping he would get to take a dip in Scary Pool.

Petunia waved to Jason, who wore his hockey mask and kept his chainsaw stowed inside his desk. She waved to Johnny, who was nibbling at an itch on his furry Sasquatch foot.

Neither boy waved back to Petunia.

They didn't intend to be mean. They were just scared that it might incite the bees swarming around Petunia's head to attack. They nodded back ever so slightly, noticing Petunia's long purple hair draping down her purple shoulders and over her purple dress.

Petunia liked purple. A lot. But since she was completely purple from head to foot, she didn't really have much choice.

Fred, the boy without fear, strolled down the aisle, cool and relaxed, wearing his baggy jeans and backward cap.

Petunia noticed Lindsey, Stephanie, and Maria looking at Fred dreamily and felt a twinge of . . . something. She couldn't quite label it. Fred stopped by Johnny's desk and helped him scratch the itch with his long sharpened fingernails.

"Aaaah," said Johnny, relieved. "Thanks!"

"Ha," laughed Fred. "There's definitely no such thing as a talking Sasquatch. Looks like I'm still dreaming."

Yep, everything seemed back to normal, as if King Zog's attack on the school just a few weeks ago was a distant memory.

Suddenly, a stomping from outside shook the room. It was the warning

that their teacher, Mr. Grump, was approaching. Petunia hoped his memory had improved enough over the break that he would at least remember he was the teacher.

As Mr. Grump stomped into the room, everyone rushed to their seats. He was a very nice teacher, but the class knew that if a lagoon creature with the head of an elephant got angry, he'd have no problem charging at them, tusks first.

Mr. Grump seemed puzzled as he looked at the students. No surprise there. Puzzled was the most common expression on his face. He looked at a piece of paper in his hand. Then he looked back at the students. It was obvious he had no idea who or where he was. Then he stomped down the aisle and took a seat at one of the open desks. The chair was way too small for him and it shattered into a thousand pieces as soon as he sat on it.

"Ouch!" said Mr. Grump. "I have splinters in my bottom."

Petunia rolled her eyes and went over to help him up. She was the only student who he could consistently remember.

"Hello, Petunia," said Mr. Grump with a smile.

"Hi, Mr. Grump. You shouldn't be sitting there. You're the teacher. Remember?"

"No, I don't think so," Mr. Grump replied. "Look."

Mr. Grump handed Petunia the piece of paper.

"What does it say?" asked Wendy Crumkin, the smartest girl in class. She brushed back her red hair and pushed up her glasses over her freckled nose.

Petunia responded, "It's a note from Principal Headcrusher. It says, 'Dear Mr. Grump. It has come to my attention that you know absolutely nothing and are therefore not qualified to be a teacher at this school. However, you are welcome to join your class as a student. As soon as you know *something* instead of *nothing*, I will consider rehiring you. Yours truly, Principal Meredith Headcrusher.'"

Ramon, the zombie kid, blurted, "But . . . if he's not the teacher, then who—" Ramon's zombie jaw fell off his face in the middle of his sentence. He quickly scooped it off the ground and reattached it. "Sorry. As

I was saying . . . then who is the teacher?"

The clock struck eight a.m., and a cackling was heard from outside the door. "Heh-heh-heh-heh-heh!"

The students looked at one another and gulped. The identity of their teacher was going to be a surprise, and nobody liked surprises at Scary School. If you were the recipient of a surprise, the bigger surprise would be if you still had all your arms and legs a moment later.

Suddenly, the door was kicked open, and an old man wearing a long white lab coat stumbled into the classroom. In his arms he carried dozens of beakers and jars full of colorful bubbling chemicals.

The beakers and jars were piled so high they nearly touched the ceiling. They wobbled back and forth and looked like they were about to come crashing down at any moment.

The items were blocking the teacher's face, so nobody could tell who it was. But then the teacher set the beakers down on his desk and emerged from behind them.

"Hello, class!" exclaimed the teacher in a high-pitched, maniacal voice. "I'm baaaack!"

The entire class screamed at the same time. Penny Possum fell to the ground and played dead.

It was Mr. Acidbath.

2

Charles Nukid's Worst Day Ever

At the same time Petunia's class was screaming at the sight of Mr. Acidbath, Charles Nukid was sitting in King Khufu's classroom with his head buried in his arms, wiping away tears with his polka-dot tie. As usual, he was the only student wearing the uniform of gray shorts, a white dress shirt, and that ridiculous tie.

Ever since he and Penny Possum had begun their

friendship by giving each other a piece of candy every day, they had met each morning at the front entrance of the school to throw a crab into the moat for Archie the Giant Squid.

Today, Charles had waited for Penny as long as he could, but she never showed. Charles thought she might be out sick, but then he saw her slipping into her classroom before the morning bell. She must have taken one of the secret entrances to avoid him.

He couldn't stop thinking about what had happened the day before, which was undoubtedly the worst day of his life.

Yesterday morning, he called Penny on the phone and said, "Hey, Penny, if you're free today, do you want to go sledding?"

Penny didn't answer him and Charles smiled. That, of course, meant yes. Penny hardly ever spoke, but when she needed to say no, she said no.

"Okay, then," Charles responded. "I'll meet you at noon."

"(Silence)," Penny replied.

"Oh, okay, one o'clock at Goblin Hill?"

"(Silence)."

"I'm looking forward to it, too. Good-bye!"

Charles had gotten very good at interpreting

Penny's silences. He was so excited that when he hung up the phone, he started jumping for joy on his bed. Then he remembered that jumping on his bed was against the rules. He hopped off, fixed the bedding, and gave himself a five-minute time-out.

The sun was shining brightly in the sky. Charles's amazing luck seemed to be continuing. After miraculously leading the students of Scary School to victory over ten thousand monsters the day before winter break, he had become the school hero. And now he was going to celebrate the New Year with his best friend, Penny. If he was lucky, maybe he'd even get a hug at the end of the day.

Penny reached the peak of Goblin Hill at precisely one o'clock. Charles was already waiting for her, holding two cups of hot cocoa and a picnic basket full of goodies. She was wearing a brand-new yellow sweater that she had just gotten for Christmas. Charles thought she looked like a sunrise coming over the hill.

A band of goblins was standing behind Charles. Each one was holding a different instrument—there was a flautist goblin, a guitarist goblin, a drummer goblin, and a triangle goblin.

When the band saw Penny, they quickly broke into song on Charles's cue, but, as usual, they had not bothered to rehearse and were playing all the wrong notes. Goblins are terrible musicians, but that never seems to stop them.

Charles and Penny sat on their sleds atop the hill, sipping the hot cocoa and admiring the breathtaking view. They could see all of Scary School, which looked not-quite-as-deady in its peaceful state during winter break. They could see the rustling trees of Scary Forest, the murky depths of Scary Pool, and the screaming face of Petrified Pavilion.

After finishing the cocoa, Penny pulled a box out of her jacket. On the label it read POSSUM'S HOT PEPPERS. She poured a bunch of green, red, and orange peppers into Charles's hands. A fly landed on one of the orange peppers and exploded. Charles gulped.

Penny took a green pepper and popped it in her mouth. She encouraged Charles to do the same. Charles had never tasted a hot pepper before, and he was kind of scared. But since Penny's family grew the peppers, he didn't want to insult her.

They bit down on the green peppers together. It felt like fireworks were going off inside Charles's mouth. But after a few moments the heat went away, and it actually tasted pretty good.

"I like it!" said Charles, his eyes watering from the heat. Penny looked impressed.

Next, Charles reached for one of the orange peppers. Penny quickly grabbed his hand and shook her head.

Charles didn't like Penny thinking he wasn't tough enough to eat a tiny little pepper.

"Don't worry," said Charles. "I can totally handle it."

Penny gave him one last look that seemed to say, "Are you sure about this?"

Penny let go of his hand. Charles reached for the orange pepper. The skin of the pepper was sweating. Steam rose from the stem. If it could talk, it would be screaming, "Don't eat me!"

Charles slowly put the pepper between his teeth and bit down.

He put on a brave face and tried to smile through the blazing inferno that had just exploded in his mouth. His tongue felt like he had licked a pool of lava. Tears were streaming down his face like rain on a windowpane.

Penny saw that he was not a happy camper, but she was amazed he was holding himself together.

Thinking the worst was over, Charles swallowed it down in one gulp, but without the saliva to keep his mouth cool, the heat suddenly intensified fifty times. The world became blurry, and Charles couldn't hold back any longer. He screamed, "AAAAIIIIEEEEE!" and he ran around in circles hoping the wind might cool his mouth. It didn't.

Penny was cracking up.

"Water!" Charles begged.

Penny pointed to a patch of snow nearby.

Charles scooped up the snow and shoveled it into his mouth. But instead of helping, the snow spread the heat all over his insides. Penny fell over in silent laughter. Charles then remembered that there's just one thing that cools down spicy food.

"Milk!" screamed Charles, jumping up and down and spinning in circles.

Penny shrugged her shoulders. She didn't have any.

Charles realized he had only one option to extinguish the blaze.

He reached into his picnic basket and pulled out a banana whipped cream pie. The white foam resting on top of the creamy filling looked like an oasis.

Penny's jaw dropped when she realized what Charles was about to do. Charles didn't waste another moment. He smashed the pie straight into his own face.

Charles inhaled the creamy foam, and the cooling relief was immediate. He kept the pie on his face for almost a minute, basking in the frosty frosting until he had to come out for air.

His face was covered in the white foam, but he could still hear Penny's muffled giggles. He realized how silly he must look and started laughing along with her.

But then Penny's laugh changed from a girlish "hee-hee-hee" to a monstrous "har-har-har!"

Charles wiped the pie off his face and noticed with horror that a seventh-grade troll—the captain of the Scary School football team—was holding Penny over his head.

"Come get your girlfriend!" mocked the troll.

"She's not my girlfriend, Lebok," said Charles, "but put her down anyway!"

"Or else what?" laughed Lebok. "What you gonna do?"

Another seventh-grade troll named Padlox stomped up behind Charles and barked, "Me and Lebok need hill to throw football. You two go bye-byes."

"No," said Charles. "I reserved the hill for today. Ask the goblins."

Padlox retorted, "Goblins? What they do? Sing me to death?"

"Hey!" shouted the goblins, a little insulted.

Charles sighed and lowered his head. There was nothing he could do. The trolls were as big as gorillas and twice as strong. If they wanted the hill, it was theirs.

"Fine," said Charles. "We'll leave. Just put her down."

"Wise choice, human."

Lebok put Penny down on the blanket, but she was not ready to give up. Fuming mad, she shouted

"No!" at the trolls, thinking her booming voice could knock them out. But the trolls were like trees and hardly budged. Then she charged at Lebok and started pounding him with her fists. It was like hitting a brick wall.

"Har-har! Stop that, human girl. You tickling me!"

Penny continued pounding him, until Lebok got annoyed and pushed her away. Penny fell backward into a pit of mud. Charles pulled her out, but her new yellow sweater was completely ruined.

The trolls sniggered. "Har-har-har! That's what you get for messing with trolls!"

Penny glared at Charles. Her eyes were screaming to him, "Do something!"

"What can I do? Monster Math won't work on those trolls because they're too dumb to know the difference between big numbers and small ones."

Penny raised her fists, urging Charles to challenge the trolls.

"I can't fight them. Fighting other students is against the rules."

Penny rolled her eyes, completely fed up. Charles tried to take her hand, but Penny pushed Charles away. He stumbled backward, falling into the mud pit himself.

Lebok and Padlox gobbled Charles's lunch and passed the football. "Bye-bye, puny humans!"

Still fuming, Penny ran off, leaving Charles in the mud pit. As he sat there dumbfounded, the brief winter sunshine disappeared, dark clouds moved in, and a light snow began to fall.

Now sitting in class the following day, Charles regretted not standing up for Penny. At the time, he blamed it on the rules, but the truth was he had been afraid. Frozen with fear, he could only watch as the mean troll had shoved Penny into the mud. What rule could he possibly have broken to deserve this?

At eight a.m., class was about to start. Charles sat up at his desk as vampire kid Bryce McCallister and the brave Steven Kingsley kicked the golden sarcophagus in the shins. It creaked open, and King Khufu emerged with a menacing groan from his winter hibernation, filling the room with his dank five-thousand-year-old mummy breath.

Dusting off his ancient bandages, King Khufu muttered in his gravelly, sandy voice, "I trust you all had a fun vacation. I myself had a wonderful time playing with Kitty Tut."

Kitty Tut was King Khufu's mummified cat. It had

not come back to life like King Khufu had. It was planted atop King Khufu's desk with a frozen look of shock on its face.

"Who's a good kitty?" King Khufu cooed, scratching behind its ear, which subsequently broke off. "Aww. Did somebody lose an ear? We'll have to get you a new one right away!"

The students quickly covered their ears.

That's when Charles felt a thousand legs crawling up his arm that would change his life forever.

3

Ninjas Never Laugh

"Agh!" Charles yelped. Slinking up his arm was a seven-inch-long black millipede. From Charles's zoological studies, he knew they were highly poisonous.

"You need not fear Millie. She bites only on my command," said a girl seated next to him. Every inch of her was covered in a black ninja outfit known as a *shinobi shozoku*. I know that because (as you may remember from reading my author bio on the jacket) I planned on becoming a master ninja before I turned into a ghost. Even her face was hidden. He could have sworn she wasn't there a moment ago.

"Is, uh, this your millipede?" Charles asked nervously as the creature crawled up his shoulder and circled his pencil-thin neck like spaghetti wrapping around a breadstick.

"Millie is my companion."

Charles knew millipedes liked to eat vegetables. He took a carrot from his backpack and offered it to the millipede, which was now creeping up his chin and seemed to be considering burrowing inside his nose.

The millipede stopped in her tracks and sniffed the tip of the carrot. Instead of taking a nibble, the millipede stretched her mouth open to the size of a tennis ball and devoured the entire carrot in one gulp.

"Millie likes carrots," said the girl in black.

Millie gave Charles a kiss on the nose. Charles had never been kissed by anything with so many legs before. It tickled.

King Khufu was calling attendance. "McCallister?"

"My body is here, but my heart is with my true love," said Bryce McCallister with a smoldering gaze. All the girls sighed at his vampire charm.

"Nukid?"

"Here," said Charles. He turned back to the girl in black. "So, what is your name?" he asked.

"Lat—" she began.

Suddenly, the PA crackled, and the voice of Principal Headcrusher rang through the classroom. "Attention, everyone!"

The girl in black perked up in her seat, as if sensing danger. Her eyes darted and she sniffed the air. "Watch Millie," she said to Charles. Then she leaped out of her chair, sprang off the wall, and dove through the air conditioning vent in one astonishingly swift movement.

"Um . . . see ya," said Charles to her empty desk.

Principal Headcrusher continued, "After your first class, everyone is to report immediately to Petrified Pavilion for an urgent assembly. If you brought jackets or sweaters with you today, make sure to bring them. That is all."

King Khufu resumed taking roll. "Lattie?" There was no response. "Lattie . . . There is no last name. How odd."

"Um," said Charles, "I think she was here a second ago, but she dove through the air vent."

"Preposterous," said King Khufu. "I would have noticed."

"She did it *really* fast," said Charles.

"Not a chance. I'm marking her absent. Lastly . . . Tanya Tarantula?"

Tanya the Giant Tarantula raised four of her eight legs from her terrarium at the back of the classroom.

"Perfect. Now let's get started with our lesson on ancient prophecies. Please open your textbooks to page thirty-two—the Wise Wizard's Prophecy. This prophecy is of particular importance because it is scheduled to come true next week. It states that a human child will battle the scariest monster in the world to decide the fate of all monsterkind. Luckily for you human students, there are currently no signs that this prophecy will come true."

As the students began reading about the prophecy, which was written in Egyptian hieroglyphs, Lattie dropped back into her seat. This time Khufu noticed.

"Who are you?" Khufu asked the girl.

"I am the shadow in the darkness. I am the eagle on the mountain face. I am the last vision seen by an evildoer."

"Ah, you must be Lattie," said Khufu. "Where were you when I called your name?"

"The best way to tell when a ninja is here is when she is *not* here."

King Khufu fumed, "How dare you leave my class without permission! I ought to put a curse on you right here!"

Lattie responded calmly, "He who becomes angry boards a train to a wilderness of ignorance."

King Khufu was stunned that someone had dared talk back to him. The last one who did that was Eddie Bookman. As you may remember from the last book, he doesn't exist anymore.

King Khufu could only babble, "Hubble . . . habble . . . huffle . . . well, just don't do it again. Since you're new, this is your one warning."

Charles extended his arm, and the millipede used it like a bridge to crawl onto Lattie's shoulder. Lattie nodded a silent thank-you. She wasn't sure what it was, but there was something different about Charles, as if he reminded her of someone she liked, but she couldn't think who.

When King Khufu turned around to resume his

lesson, Larry Ledfoot stood up and shouted, "Hey, Toothpick!"

Larry held up a straw and shot a spitball right at Charles's face. Charles closed his eyes, dreading the embarrassment before it even hit, but he never felt the wet impact.

He opened his eyes and saw Lattie holding the spitball between the tips of two pencils, like chopsticks. She had caught it in midair just inches from his nose.

Lattie glared at Larry, then shot the spitball back at him with a flick of her wrist. It hit him right in the forehead. *Splat!*

The whole class laughed and applauded. Even King Khufu. Even Larry for that matter. It was that incredible.

Charles said to Lattie, "Thanks. I'm Charles Nukid."

"You're welcome, Charles Nukid. I am the unseen hand of righteousness. But you can call me Lattie."

Mr. Acidbath

4
The World's Scariest Teacher

Back in the other class, as soon as I saw Mr. Acidbath, I shrieked so loudly that my ghostly form became visible right next to Fritz. He got double-scared and passed out.

Penny Possum was still lying stiff as stone on the floor, playing dead.

Mr. Acidbath was the teacher whose experiment with Fear Gas had gone terribly wrong when I was still alive, turning me into the friendly ghost you know today.

"I know you probably weren't expecting me back so soon," said Mr. Acidbath in his high-pitched voice, "but I paid a visit to the All-Knowing Monkey of Scary Mountain. He divulged to me the secret to a speedy recovery from Fear Gas burns, and wowzy-woozy did it ever work! So here I am! Heh-heh-heh!"

Mr. Acidbath's cackle confirmed that he was completely out of his mind. His long white hair stretched upward, outward, and sideward above his thick goggles. His goggles protected his bulging eyeballs. His eyeballs danced in different directions.

Back when Mr. Acidbath was teaching, Petunia could hear explosions echoing from his classroom every five minutes like clockwork. She was muttering in her chair, "Please don't do an experiment. Please don't do an experiment."

"For our first experiment," said Mr. Acidbath, "I thought I would pick up where I left off and show you how to make some . . . Fear Gas!"

"Noooo!" the class hollered in unison.

"Heh-heh-heh! No need to be afraid. Well, not yet anyway. The Fear Gas will take care of that."

The class turned to Fred. He wasn't looking like his cool relaxed self at all. His eyes were glazed. His forehead was sweating. He looked . . . scared?

Mr. Acidbath walked up to the pile of chemicals on the desk. They were still wobbling precariously as he rolled up his sleeves and reached into the pile, swiftly pulling out two beakers of liquids. The class held their breath as the rest of the chemicals slipped and tumbled on top of one another, shifting positions, clanking and clattering, molding into a new shape, yet somehow maintaining their structural integrity.

The class exhaled in unison.

"Everyone, open your chemistry textbooks and take careful notes, or you might make a mistake and kill us all."

The students put their pencils to their notebooks, prepared to write down every word.

In one hand, Mr. Acidbath held up a jar of bubbling blue liquid. In the other hand, he held up a beaker of oozing red slime.

"This blue substance is the boiling tears of a bearodactyl. In this hand I hold griffin grease, mixed with some hot lava from the school's playground. Watch carefully as we make . . . Fear Gas!"

Mr. Acidbath began to pour the red slime into the jar of blue bearodactyl tears. It oozed painfully slowly. The class braced themselves as the slime inched closer to the blue tears. Even Mr. Grump covered his elephant eyes with his trunk. But as long as fearless Fred was in the room, the class knew he would save them if it went wrong.

Then Fred cried out: "Oh my gosh! This isn't a dream, is it? This is all real! Aaaaagh!"

Uh oh, everyone thought to themselves. We're in deeeeep trouble.

Fred picked the worst possible moment to have that shocking realization. Now who would save them if Mr. Acidbath's experiment went terribly wrong (as his experiments always did)?

Stunned by Fred's scream, Mr. Acidbath hollered back, "Silence! This takes perfect concentration! Exactly one drop of lava with griffin grease has to fall into the tears for this to work properly. If two drops fall in, we're all doomed! Heh-heh-heh!"

Everyone covered their mouths so not a peep would escape.

The red slime reached the tip of the beaker and began its slow descent into the bearodactyl tears, like super-thick maple syrup oozing out of a bottle. Hanging by a thin thread, it was about to break off as one drop, when suddenly the PA crackled, and the voice of Principal Headcrusher rang through the classroom. "Attention, everyone!"

The noise startled Mr. Acidbath, and a giant glob of the grease plopped out of the jar. If just two drops caused the last Fear Gas explosion, this would be enough to blow up the entire school.

Everyone, including Fred, dove under their desks and covered their heads.

"I repeat! Attention all students and faculty of Scary School," Principal Headcrusher continued. "This is Principal Headcrusher."

There was silence in the classroom. When no explosion happened, the class raised their heads over their desks.

"Wowzy-woozy! That was close! Looks like we have a new class hero," Mr. Acidbath announced.

Mr. Acidbath pointed upward where Lattie—the girl in black—was hanging from the rafters by her feet, clutching the jar of bubbling blue tears. He exclaimed, "That girl appeared out of nowhere and pulled the jar away at the last moment!"

The red slime had burned a basketball-sized hole

through the teacher's desk and was sizzling on the floor. "Let's all give her a big thank-you."

Before anyone could say thank you, the girl in black, still hanging upside down on the rafters, stated, "One who receives kindness should never forget it. One who performs kindness should never remember it."

The students looked at one another and scratched their heads, trying to figure out what that meant.

Principal Headcrusher's announcement continued: "After class, everyone is to report immediately to Petrified Pavilion for an urgent assembly. If you brought jackets or sweaters with you today, make sure to bring them. That is all."

By the way, you read about Principal Headcrusher's announcement twice because I was floating between the walls of each classroom the moment it happened. That's how I know what was happening in two places at once. If you ever notice weird things that don't make sense, just remember, I'm a ghost. I can do lots of crazy stuff.

"Looks like our experiment will have to wait until after the assembly," said Mr. Acidbath with a disappointed look. "Hopefully there won't be any more slipups, but I can't make any promises. Heh-heh-heh!

Then one of the beakers of chemicals fell through the hole in the desk. The wobbling tower swayed to the right. *Gasp!* Then it swayed to the left. *Gasp!* Then it came crashing down to a cacophony of breaking glass.

"Holy cannoli! Get out of here quick!" Mr. Acidbath ordered.

The class immediately bolted out of the door as a rainbow of gases started snaking around the room, causing kids to cough, burp, and sneeze violently. Luckily, the last kid dove out of the room safely as Mr. Acidbath slammed the door shut.

Through the window in the doorway, the class watched as the gases interacted, causing booming colorful explosions. A thick cloud formed on the ceiling. Then it started to rain a sparkling green substance that burned tiny holes in everyone's desks, turning each one into Swiss cheese.

Mr. Acidbath cackled, "Wowzy-woozy! I hope you all brought your acid-proof umbrellas today. Heh-heh-heh! I love science!"

5

The Snowman Cometh

The students of Scary School commenced the usual procedure for assembly. They gathered upon the vast wooden hands of Petrified Pavilion and were fed into its eternally screaming mouth—the only permissible means of entry into its grand hall.

The first thing the students noticed when they entered the pavilion was that it felt like a freezer. Usually it's much warmer inside than outside on a winter day, but today it was like walking into a meat locker.

In the bleachers, everyone was shivering and huddling together for warmth. Their combined breath formed a fine mist that hung above their heads. The kids prayed they wouldn't end up frozen.

Charles Nukid searched the crowd for Penny in hopes that they might get to sit together, but Penny was with her class at the opposite side of the pavilion. She didn't seem to be looking for him. Charles grimaced and huddled next to his friend Bryce McCallister, whose cold vampire body wasn't any help.

Principal Headcrusher, with her frizzy black hair and hands the size of Hula-Hoops, stepped up to the podium and raised her palms to her mouth. All the students quickly stuck their fingers in their ears so that their eardrums wouldn't explode.

"Good morning, students. I'm happy to say that I have a wonderful surprise for all of you."

The students said a silent good-bye to their vital appendages.

"For the first time, Scary School has been invited to participate in a student exchange program with another school in the Scary community. Six students will be chosen to spend a week at Scream Academy, my proud alma mater, widely regarded as the scariest school in the world. The students chosen will be those who not only have the best chance at survival but who also best represent the human race.

Every kid hoped they would *not* be the ones chosen to go.

"I have been assured that this exchange has absolutely *nothing* to do with the Wise Wizard's Prophecy that a human child will have to battle the scariest monster in the world to decide the fate of all monsterkind. So no need to worry about that."

Everyone looked around at one another, clearly worried about that.

"The selector of those lucky six students is none other than the principal of Scream Academy, who will be staying with us for the week and observing all of you very closely. Would you like to meet him?"

All the students shook their heads no.

"Too bad! Please give a very cold round of applause for the abominable snowman himself, Principal Rolf Meltington!" Principal Headcrusher turned to the side and yodeled, "Snowa-lowa-lay-hee-hoo!"

The side door flung open, and a blizzard of snow flew into the pavilion. The frost whipped through the hall like a flying avalanche. Zombie kid Benny Porter had forgotten his beanie and keeled over from zombie brain freeze. Nurse Hairymoles had to quickly turn him into an ice monster to save him. Benny learned a very valuable life lesson about not forgetting to bring his beanie to school. Of course it was too late to apply that lesson, but it was learned nonetheless.

The snow settled behind the podium and began to form itself into Principal Meltington—the abominable snowman. The students gasped when they saw him. They thought he would look like a furry white Sasquatch, but he looked more like an actual snowman that had come to life. Instead of a big ball of snow for his lower section, he had thick snow legs. His arms were jagged tree branches. He sported a black stovepipe hat, a long carrot nose, and button eyes, and his mouth looked like it was scooped out of his face.

When he spoke into the podium microphone, his voice sounded deep and ominous, like a roll of thunder in the far distance.

"Thank you, Principal Headcrusher. And thank you to the students for accommodating my climatological needs. The pavilion is a little warm for my taste, but I don't think I'll be melting anytime soon."

The students' teeth were chattering, and icicles were hanging from their noses. He wanted it colder?

"I'll make this brief so you won't turn into human Popsicles before my button eyes. As I observe you this

week, please don't do anything out of the ordinary or feel the need to impress me. Simply be yourselves, and that will be the best way for me to judge who is worthy of visiting Scream Academy, which, as Principal Headcrusher said, has *nothing* to do with the terrible prophecy that a human child will have to battle the scariest monster of all time next week. Remember to bring your warmest clothes, as this bitter cold follows me wherever I go. Also, I will need a fresh carrot each morning to replace my nose or else I won't be able to properly smell your fear. Principal Headcrusher is the only human to ever attend Scream Academy, and perhaps she has proven with this school that more human children will be able to attend in the future. Nobody thinks you have a chance of survival, but hopefully you'll prove them wrong. Have an 'ice' day."

Principal Meltington paused for laughter at his pun. Nobody laughed. So he said it again in a more ominous voice. "Have an *ice . . . day*!" The students realized he wasn't going to leave until they laughed, so they chuckled politely, pretending to just get it.

Satisfied, Principal Meltington waved his arms and turned himself back into a blizzard, but before flying off, Meltington's head popped out and said, "Oh, I almost forgot. Have any of you ever battled a dragon as large as a mountain?"

Everyone gulped. A mountain? The largest dragon any of them had ever seen was Dr. Dragonbreath, and he was only nine feet. And no one would battle him for a million dollars!

Seeing not a single hand raised, Meltington said, "Ah, well, that's a shame. Again, *nothing* to do with the prophecy." The doors swung open, and the snow that filled the pavilion lifted up and flew out the door with Meltington.

The students would have applauded, but their arms were frozen stiff.

"That's all. Back to your classes!" proclaimed Principal Headcrusher.

The students of Mr. Acidbath's class couldn't decide whether they preferred to stay in the pavilion and freeze to death or go back to class and deal with the acid rain.

Sometimes life comes down to a choice of the lesser of two evils. Like who to vote for in a class election when you don't like either kid running. It was a tough call, but the students decided to head back to class, where they could at least face their doom with warm hearts and minds.

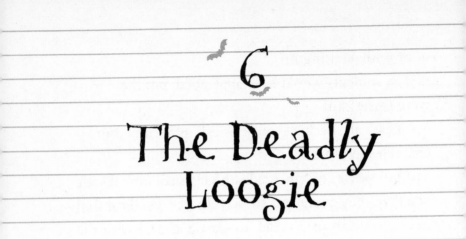

6

The Deadly Loogie

The rule at Scary School is that once the class bell rings, every student must be inside his or her classroom. Nobody, not even a teacher, is allowed to be wandering the hallways, or else the hall monitor, Ms. Hydra, is welcome to make a meal of you.

Rules are rules.

Mr. Acidbath's class stood outside his classroom and peered inside. The acid rain had turned into an acid storm, and everything inside the classroom had all but disintegrated.

"That storm looks incredibly deadly," said Frank, which is pronounced "Rachel."

"Hey! Don't judge the storm by its looks," said Lindsey.

"Mr. Acidbath, can't you get rid of the acid rain?" Petunia asked.

"Nope!" said Mr. Acidbath with a grin. "I don't even know why it's happening! Heh-heh-heh! Sorry to laugh. It's all I can do when I'm scared out of my mind!"

"Well," said Johnny the Sasquatch, "we have about thirty seconds before the bell rings and Ms. Hydra eats us all."

Peter (the nicest kid in school) transformed into Peter the Wolf (the meanest kid in school) and growled, "Don't be chicken, guys! We can take Ms. Hydra!"

"I don't think so," said Wendy Crumkin. "Ms. Hydra is a twenty-foot monitor lizard with nine heads. She's eaten entire armies without breaking a sweat. If we get eaten, there's no coming back."

Jason exclaimed, "Come on, guys. We need ideas, fast!"

Mr. Grump raised his hand.

"Yes, Mr. Grump?"

"Who am I?"

"No time to explain!"

"We could eat the storm's braaaains!" said Ramon the Zombie.

"Too ridiculous."

"(Silence)," suggested Penny Possum.

"That's the best idea so far," said Johnny. "Which isn't saying much."

Then the class bell rang.

The classroom doors all slammed shut in unison, and after a moment of silence, the sound of hissing filled the air. It was the unmistakable sound of Ms. Hydra smelling the air with her nine tongues. Did you know monitor lizards smell with their tongues? Weird but useful! Tongues can't get stuffy.

"I ssssmell fresh children in the hallwaysssss." Her slithery voice echoed from around the corner.

"Yesss, and lots of them," said a different head.

"Shouldn't we wash our hands before we eat them?" said another head.

"No," the other heads reminded her. "We don't use our hands to eat!"

"Oh, yeah."

The nine heads of Ms. Hydra peered from around the corner, one on top of the other.

"Hello, children. I take it none of you have a hall passss?"

The students shook their heads.

"What a pity. It seemssss as though you're all breaking the rules. Ssssorry to have to eat you, but it is my job."

Ms. Hydra rushed toward them from the end of the hallway, all nine of her lizard heads bearing their razor sharp teeth.

That's when the idea came to Petunia.

"Rachel!" she shouted, speaking to Frank. "What was that noise that Principal Headcrusher made to summon Principal Meltington?"

"I don't remember. It was some kind of yodel."

"Right! I think it was . . ." Petunia stepped forward and sang: "Snowa-lowa-lay-hee-hoo!"

In an instant, a blizzard of snow streamed through the hallway. It hit Ms. Hydra right as she was about to chomp on Fritz's head. Ms. Hydra froze in midair, enveloped in a giant block of ice as she fell to the floor.

"Quick!" shouted Petunia. "Into the classroom!"

The students rushed inside the classroom as the snowy blizzard followed after them. The drops of acid rain stung their skin, but only a few drops had hit each student before the blizzard extinguished the burning acid and turned it into a harmless green snow.

The snow then rose up into the snowman form of Principal Meltington. Once himself, Principal Meltington made a snorting sound. All of the green acid formed into a slimy ball in his mouth, and he spit it out across the room in dramatic fashion, sending it crashing through the window and landing with a splash in Scary Fountain. From that day forward, taking a dip in Scary Fountain would result in hideous mutations.

The class erupted in cheers. They all ran up and hugged Petunia, not caring if they got stung by the bees around her head.

As Principal Meltington approached Petunia, the rest of the class backed away.

"Are you the one who summoned me?" he asked, his deep voice shaking the room.

"Y-y-yes," answered Petunia. "Sorry."

"Don't be. That was some very quick thinking. Scream Academy–type of quick thinking," he added with a wink of his button eye.

Great, thought Petunia. Now I'm sure to get picked for the exchange.

When the lunch bell rang that afternoon, King Khufu went back into his sarcophagus, and his students quickly packed up their things for lunch. But when they opened the classroom door, they were met with a big surprise.

They were snowed in.

It looked like there had been an avalanche in the hallway during class. There was no way out. The desperate students tried digging and clawing at the snow, but their small hands made little progress.

They looked out the window. It was a fifty-foot drop to the ground below. If King Khufu were still there, perhaps they could have used his mummy bandages to rappel down the side of the building, but once he locked himself inside his sarcophagus for lunch, there was no getting him out.

Today was a special lunch day. Sue the Amazing Octo-Chef was preparing a celebratory feast in honor of Principal Meltington's arrival. It was called "The Feast of the Four Towers." One tower was to be a twenty-foot mountain of pizza. There was also going to be a tower of garlic bread, a tower of corn on the cob, and the last tower was to be a twenty-foot castle of chocolate cake. Each tower would be molded to look like one of the great towers of Scream Academy.

Nobody wanted to miss this lunch.

"We have to get out of here," Steven Kingsley screamed. "My claustrophobia is coming back! And my snowophobia!"

Larry Ledfoot tried kicking the avalanche with his stone feet, but that just packed it in worse.

Bryce McCallister tried melting the snow with his searing vampire gaze, but that didn't work either.

Charles sat at his desk, racking his brain as his

classmates screamed for help and pounded on the snow wall. The only other student not freaking out was Lattie. She was sitting on top of her desk, quietly meditating. Her millipede sat on her shoulder curled in a ball, meditating with her.

"Any ideas?" Charles asked her.

Lattie spoke, "Calmness overcomes panic as a gentle breeze tames a churning ocean."

I guess not, thought Charles.

Then Lattie added in a voice that sounded like it was channeled from far away, "When deciding your future, look to the good deeds of your past."

Those words struck Charles immediately. Perhaps something he did in the past was the key to escaping the room. But what good deeds had he done? He had saved Princess Zogette in Monster

Forest. He had faced down the monster army. But something told him the answer wasn't in one of these epic events. It had to be simpler.

He searched his thoughts. What was the last good deed I performed? I guess it was feeding Millie the piece of carrot.

"Oh my gosh. That's it!" Charles shouted. "Lattie, may I borrow Millie?"

"Ask her yourself."

Charles extended his hand to Millie. She uncurled from her ball and crawled up Charles's arm, tickling him like crazy. He had to bite his lip not to laugh.

Charles looked around and found some string in his desk. He brought Millie to the avalanche, tied a carrot from his lunch bag to the end of the piece of string, and hung the carrot in front of Millie. The millipede lunged toward it with a violent chomp. Charles pulled the carrot away at the last second. The millipede got a mouthful of snow and spit it out. Aggravated, the millipede continued chomping away as Charles dangled the carrot in front of her.

Within minutes, a tunnel had formed through the snow. Being the skinniest kid in school, Charles was just able to fit through the tunnel. Millie continued gnashing away at the snow until they reached the other end.

Lattie followed behind Charles, widening the tunnel with motorlike ninja chops for the rest of the class to follow after her.

When they popped out the other side, Charles and Lattie fell to the floor. Crazed with hunger, Millie devoured the carrot in one gulp and released a loud belch. Charles laughed, but Lattie didn't make a sound because ninjas never laugh.

When the pair looked up, they saw Principal Meltington standing before them.

"Very impressive," he said to both of them, making a note in his snow book. "Scream Academy impressive."

Charles smacked his head. Now I'm going to get picked to go to Scream Academy for sure, he thought. Rumor had it that Scream Academy had no rules whatsoever, and he wanted nothing to do with a place like that.

King Khufu's class ran to the lunch and made it just in time for the four-tower feast. Charles and Lattie had a wonderful time trying to see who could eat more of the chocolate walls before the end of lunch. Pretty soon, the walls got so thin that the whole fluffy castle collapsed on top of them, and they had an even better time eating their way out.

Principal Meltington thought, I suppose I made those first tests far too easy. But tomorrow they'll be lucky to make it through their classes in one piece.

7

Fred's Silver Hammer

On Thursday morning, the students arrived at school and found that an enormous block of ice had sealed the entrance. The trolls couldn't budge it, nor could the werewolves cut it with their claws.

If they were standing out on the front lawn when class started, it would spell certain doom. The vicious gargoyles were always on the lookout for students outside during class hours.

Luckily, Jason was on hand with his trusty chainsaw.

As his chainsaw whirred, everyone backed out of the way. With the precision of a craftsman, Jason sculpted the ice block into a perfect sculpture of Ms. Fangs.

The students cheered Jason's fine work. It looked exactly like her! Everyone gave Jason exuberant high fives as they walked past the sculpture and squeezed through the entrance doors.

Ms. Fangs would never get to see the sculpture, since it was standing out in the sun. However, the gym teacher, Mr. Snakeskin, liked the sculpture so much he offered to buy it from Jason for a hundred dollars. Jason accepted in a heartbeat.

Unfortunately, the sculpture had melted by noon, and all that was left was a puddle on the ground. Mr. Snakeskin was dumbfounded and tried to get his money back.

"Sorry," said Jason. "Caveat emptor. May the buyer beware!"

Mr. Snakeskin sneered. He learned a valuable life lesson about not buying ice sculptures. Then he swept up the liquid remains into a glass jar and placed it on his shelf. He labeled the jar of water: MS. FANGS. When kids see it sitting in his office, they think it's really weird.

On Friday morning, the students discovered that the entire front lawn of Scary School was now covered in a thin layer of ice. Padlox the Troll tried to walk across but fell right through into a lake of freezing water. His buddy, Lebok, fished him out just in time, before he turned into an ice cube.

Some of the lighter third-grade students tried tiptoeing across the ice, but it started cracking. Luckily, Frank (which is pronounced "Rachel") had tied one of her invisible ropes around the youngsters' waists and yanked them off the ice before they fell through.

Petunia asked the bees if they could carry her across,

but they buzzed back, "No way! That's too far!"

Nobody could figure out how to get across, and time was running out to get into the school.

Finally, Fred stepped forward. After surviving the acid rainstorm, he was once again certain that this was all a dream. Fred confidently stepped onto the thin layer of ice.

"Don't do it!" Fred's best friend, Jason, yelled.

"It's okay, Jason," said Fred. "It's only a dream!"

The students held their breath as Fred took another step. The ice didn't break. He took another step. It still didn't break.

It turned out that Principal Meltington had created a special kind of ice that only cracked when it sensed the tremors of nervousness. Every other student was so anxious when they tried to walk across the ice that it broke apart instantly, but Fred's coolness kept the ice solid.

Fred strolled across the ice until he reached the school's front entrance. There was a magnificent silver sledgehammer waiting for him on a pedestal. It was as big as he was! As he grasped it, he realized exactly what he was supposed to do with it. He said to himself, "Oh, man. This is going to be awesome."

Fred marched down the front steps, showing off the

sledgehammer to his schoolmates across the frozen lake.

"Fred! Fred! Fred!" the school chanted.

Fred brought down the hammer with all his might upon the ice. The ice shattered into millions of tiny pieces, revealing a lake underneath. Then Principal Meltington popped up from the center of the lake holding a giant cork. A whirlpool formed at the center of the lake, draining the water underground.

"Well done!" proclaimed Principal Meltington, winking at Fred. "You may all go to your classes."

The students patted Fred on the back as they walked past him. Once again, he was the school hero.

"Thanks, everybody," he said. "This is definitely my new favorite dream!"

Once inside, the students went to their classes and enjoyed a nearly horror-free day. But Meltington surprised everyone during their final class by giving them a special pop quiz that tested their knowledge on monsters and scary creatures. No one was allowed to leave without turning it in.

Charles Nukid was thrilled to display his expertise in his favorite subject. He wrote a whole paragraph on werewolf dietary habits and a whole page on ways to create a zombie. The only part that stumped him was the section on trolls. He had never been able to find much information about them. He assumed it was because they lived in deep, dark caves that no researchers have been brave enough to enter.

As soon as he turned in the test, Charles regretted trying so hard. His effort had probably just increased his chances of being chosen for the exchange program.

When the bell rang on Friday afternoon, Charles and every other student were not happy in the least. On Monday morning, Meltington would announce which kids he had chosen to attend Scream Academy for the week.

Could you enjoy your weekend, knowing Monday could be your last day on Earth?

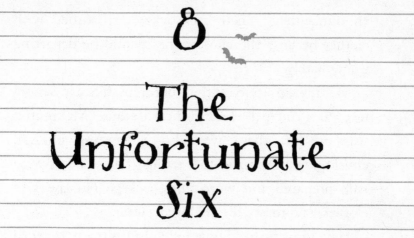

The Unfortunate Six

O ver the weekend, every student at Scary School spent quality time with their families. Charles went to the zoo with his parents. Peter the Wolf howled at the moon with his father. Penny enjoyed a delicious hot-pepper casserole with Mr. and Mrs. Possum.

Then Monday morning, instead of going to class, all the students gathered on the front lawn for the announcement. Their backpacks were stuffed with clothes because the chosen ones would be departing immediately.

Meltington stood on the front steps of Scary School next to Principal Headcrusher. Because Meltington was present, there was also a freezing blizzard enveloping a thousand-foot radius. The students were well prepared and wore thick jackets, ten layers of clothes, and toasty thermal underwear.

Hey, I just realized how much I miss toasty thermal underwear. You kids with bodies are so lucky.

"Good morning," spoke Principal Meltington in his deep, thunderous voice. "I will now announce which six students will be attending Scream Academy for the week. While many of you human students have proven yourselves worthy, the six I have chosen are the ones I believe stand the best chance of survival."

Almost every student crossed their fingers and prayed they were not worthy.

"I would like to point out that nobody expects you to survive, so don't feel bad if you don't. Principal Headcrusher is the only human student who has ever made it out alive, but of course she has a rather monstrous pair of hands, which none of you seem to have. Shame. I was hoping that was a more common trait among you humans. But if you don't make it out alive, we promise to put up a plaque in your honor in the Scream Academy Museum of Lost Souls. Sound good?"

It sounded terrible.

"All right, then. Let's get this party started. The first student I have chosen is one who showed outstanding creative thinking and remarkable skill with a chainsaw. Jason Borzees!

Jason stepped onto the platform, wearing his ever-present hockey mask and lumberjack outfit. Principal Meltington handed him an official certificate of acceptance into Scream Academy. He buzzed his chainsaw over his head, declaring, "I am honored to represent the school. If I don't make it back, I want my best friend, Fred, to take my place as goalie on the Scary School hockey team. Win the championship in my memory!"

The students cheered their hearts out.

"Funny you should mention Fred," said Principal Meltington, cutting off the cheers. "Because he showed he could remain cool and calm under the most icy of circumstances, my second choice is Fred Kroger!"

"Never mind!" said Jason. "Forfeit the hockey season in memory of Fred and me."

The students groaned.

Petunia was standing next to her best friend, Frank. They were squeezing each other's hands so tightly it was hurting, but they couldn't stop. Petunia may not have spoken very often to Jason and Fred, but they had saved her life more times than she could count.

"The third student making the trip is a girl who summoned me in order to save the lives of everyone in her class. She showed that sometimes the most courageous thing you can do is to know when to ask for help. Please join us . . . Petunia Petals!"

By the way, I know that's the first time you've heard Petunia's last name. She thinks it's silly and asked me not to put it in these books, but it was unavoidable in this circumstance. Sorry, Petunia. For the record, I really like your name.

Petunia actually smiled when she heard her name. She realized it wasn't because she wanted to go to Scream Academy, or because she would be joining Jason and Fred. It was because she didn't think she was even in the running since she's half flower and half girl, and considered a scary kid. The fact that she was human enough to be chosen for the trip made her feel less strange than she'd ever felt. She stood on the platform and was actually shedding purple tears of joy.

"My fourth choice is the one who got the highest score on the monster pop quiz."

Charles Nukid froze in fear. He wished someone were there he could hold on to, but he was alone. Penny was standing with her class. His new friend, Lattie, was nowhere in sight. However, since she's a ninja, that was the surest sign that she was somewhere near.

"The student who got the highest score on the quiz is . . . Wendy Crumkin!"

Charles breathed a sigh of relief. He was feeling two things at once: upset that someone had beaten him in his favorite subject, but glad that he hadn't been chosen.

Wendy Crumkin stepped onto the platform and bravely took her place with the other students. Standing tall, she pulled her red hair back in a ponytail, pushed up her big round glasses that rested atop her freckly nose, and smiled broadly. Of all the students, she was the only one actually excited about being chosen. If I survive, imagine how good it will look on my college applications, she was thinking.

"I have chosen the fifth student mainly because he's so skinny that he won't look very appetizing to the hungry monster students. Charles Nukid!"

Charles couldn't move. Dr. Dragonbreath had to lift Charles in his talons and fly him onto the platform.

"Thank you, Dr. Dragonbreath," said Charles.

"You can repay me by surviving," Dr. Dragonbreath replied. "I've been waiting for you to break a rule so I can gobble you up and turn you into a dragon. I'd hate to miss my chance should you perish."

Out of nowhere, a snowball hit Charles Nukid right

in the face. The crowd erupted in laughter. Wiping the snow from his eyes, Charles saw the troll Lebok high-fiving Padlox in the front row. "Good luck, Toothpick! You need it! Har-har!"

"Lastly," announced Principal Meltington, "is a student I nearly missed because she can be quite hard to spot if you're not paying close attention. A student who can remain nearly invisible is one who can do very well at Scream Academy. Please give a big cheer for the final student . . . Penny Possum!"

I know. I was thinking it was going to be Lattie too.

Penny Possum was not expecting her name to be called. All week she had purposefully avoided being noticed by Principal Meltington. Whenever she even sensed a cool breeze, she fell over and played dead.

Penny stepped onto the platform. She did not want to go Scream Academy one bit. *Especially* since Charles was going.

The only way out of it would be to play dead, and it would have to be the performance of a lifetime.

She clutched her chest like she was having a heart attack, then stumbled about the stage until she fell backward, stiffening her body into perfect rigor mortis, not moving a muscle or blinking an eyelid.

Apparently her performance was a little too dramatic because the entire school and Principal Meltington burst into applause.

"Bravo!" said Principal Meltington. "But you'll have to put on a more convincing performance in front of the monsters at Scream Academy. You'll have to join the others, unless someone worthy volunteers to go in your place."

"I volunteer!" a voice from the crowd exclaimed.

Lattie stealthily appeared next to Meltington as if she had been there the entire time.

"I'm sorry," Principal Meltington said. "But you have not proven yourself worthy in my time here. I'm afraid you may not—"

In a flash, Lattie pulled out her ninja blade and chopped the snowman's carrot nose in half. A portion flew into the air, and Lattie diced it into a dozen tiny

pieces before skewering each one on a ninja *sai*. I've asked the illustrator to draw you a picture of a *sai* in case you don't know what it looks like. Pretty cool, right?

Lattie warned, "A man who has committed a mistake and doesn't correct it is committing another mistake."

"Well," said Meltington. "I'm convinced."

Penny sprang back to life and ducked into the crowd. Lattie took her place next to Charles Nukid. She was a chilling sight in her black ninja suit.

The students cheered as loudly as they could for Jason, Fred, Petunia, Wendy, Charles, and Lattie, who were basking in the crowd's love.

In addition to their backpacks, each of the six got to choose one special item to take with them. Jason had a hard time choosing between his chainsaw and his favorite hockey stick, but he chose his hockey stick because the games in the Arctic Circle were sure to be legendary. Fred took the silver hammer, which Principal Meltington had allowed him to keep. Wendy Crumkin brought her Monster Math calculator. Petunia brought a copy of the first Scary School book to give as a present to the Scream Academy library. That way the monster kids could read it and learn about Scary School whenever they wanted.

Wasn't that thoughtful of her? Petunia is so cool.

Charles Nukid's item of choice was the present given to him by Princess Zogette—the Guitar Legend guitar signed by all the monsters of rock. Guitar Legend was the one thing Charles was really good at besides following rules, so he figured it might come in handy if he needed to impress an angry monster.

Lattie had a tough choice, but in the end she decided to leave all her ninja weapons and take Millie, her pet millipede.

Once everything was packed up, Principal Meltington proclaimed, "I'm going to get myself a new nose from the kitchen and will be meeting all six of you at Scream Academy in a few hours."

"Wait," said Petunia. "How are we getting there?"

Meltington smiled. "My dear purple girl. There's only one way to get to Scream Academy."

Suddenly, there was a loud roar from behind the unfortunate six. When they turned around and saw what was there, six earsplitting screams filled the air.

9

Into the Wolf's Mouth

At first, Charles Nukid feared that the creature standing before him was his dreaded mortal enemy—the bearodactyl. But on closer inspection, Charles realized this wasn't a bearodactyl but a beast even more unique and astonishing.

It was a polter-bear. Part polar bear. Part poltergeist.

In case you aren't familiar with poltergeists, they are a rare type of ghost that can have a physical impact in our world. When you're a regular ghost, like me, everything passes straight through you. I can't pick up a pencil or sit in a chair. But poltergeists like to scare the living by moving chairs, opening windows, or turning lights on and off. Usually they do it just for a laugh.

The polter-bears were a magnificent sight to behold. Each one looked like a polar bear, but they were way bigger. The size of a van! They were also translucent, as if they were halfway between here and not here. Sort of like a staticky TV program.

There were three polter-bears in total, and on top of each bear, a different kind of monster was sitting on a saddle.

"These three monsters were chosen from Scream Academy to spend the week at Scary School," said Principal Meltington. "There will be time for introductions later, but now, the six must be off to make it to their first class on time!"

Each monster hopped off the polter-bear and shook hands with the unfortunate six.

"Go ahead," urged Principal Meltington. "Say hello to your bear."

Normally, approaching any kind of bear is a *very* bad idea, but since polter-bears are no longer alive, they don't get hungry, so it's fairly safe.

The monsters hoisted the six onto their saddles—two kids to a bear.

Principal Headcrusher gently shook her students' hands with her thumb and index finger, taking care not to break any bones. "Good luck," she said to each of them. "And remember, no matter how dark the day becomes, your friends at Scary School are always with you."

The students of Scary School waved good-bye to the chosen six. Many were crying, thinking they would probably never be heard from again. The six waved bye back to their friends and put on brave faces, basking in the crowd's cheers. Charles searched for Penny, but before he could find her, Principal Headcrusher exclaimed, "Hee-ya!" and the polter-bears leaped off the platform. Everyone screamed because it looked like the polter-bears were going to crash into the crowd, but instead, there was a flash of light, and the bears were suddenly running up Scary Mountain.

Of course, thought Charles Nukid. Poltergeists can travel through ghost-portals! Each time a bear leaped into the air, a portal of light opened up and transported them to the next portal, like passing through one door and exiting through another door miles away.

The polter-bears lumbered up the peak, where the All-Knowing Monkey of Scary Mountain was hanging by its tail on a palm tree frond, enjoying a delicious coconut breakfast. The monkey dropped his coconut on the ground and shrieked when he saw the polter-bears galloping toward him, but then there was another flash of light, and the polter-bears were huffing across a vast open plain. They were running right next to a herd of buffalo. The buffalo got spooked and stampeded off in a different direction.

As the riders continued traveling north toward the Arctic Circle, Charles finally felt at ease enough to turn around and ask Lattie, "Why did you take Penny's place?"

Lattie answered, "Good fortune comes from selflessness. Misfortune comes from selfishness."

"What does that mean?" Charles shouted back over a gust of wind from the icy tundra they were now traversing.

Lattie sighed. "I suppose . . . I don't want you to get eaten."

"Oh," said Charles, a bit stunned. "That's the nicest thing anyone has said to me."

The weather suddenly became numbingly cold.

They had arrived at the Arctic Circle.

In the distance, three tall mountains stood in a triangle formation. Those mountains are famously known as the Three Angry Sisters. The angry sisters can be very cruel to those who attempt to scale their peaks.

The polter-bears came to an abrupt halt on a snowy terrace, then they vanished into thin air. The students fell onto the snow. Petunia noticed that all the bugs usually buzzing around her hair were gone. Bees must not like the lack of flowers in the Arctic Circle, she guessed. Jason and Fred were sad because they liked Petunia's bugs. Being friends with Petunia was like a two-for-one special. Petunia plus bugs! Every boy's dream come true.

Before them stood the four towers of Scream Academy, each composed of ice and brightly colored crystals. There was a blue tower, a pink tower, a red tower, and a green tower. The colors were meant to mirror the famous northern lights that lit the Arctic skies on many winter nights.

Ice bridges and tunnels connected each tower to caves in the mountains. Winged creatures carrying books and backpacks flew between the towers and entered the various rooms through open windows. It was a vision few humans had ever witnessed.

But the most incredible sight was the main entrance, which was an ice sculpture the size of the entire Scary School main building carved into the shape of an arctic wolf head. To enter Scream Academy, you had to walk straight into its mouth.

There's a famous Italian saying: *in bocca al lupo,* which means "into the wolf's mouth." The Italians say it to wish someone good luck. Kind of like how we say "break a leg." The meaning of the entrance was very clear. You are entering the wolf's mouth. Good luck.

Principal Meltington led the six kids into the front entrance of Scream Academy. The enormous wolf mouth came to life and snarled at them when they got close, but then Meltington threw it a meaty bone the size of a log. The mouth chomped on the treat, and its demeanor changed entirely. It licked its chops with a big icy tongue, then the tongue unfurled onto the ground so the kids could climb it and enter the main hall.

The hall was inside a dome the size of a stadium. The walls, which arched to form the ceiling, were covered with lockers. Walking creatures had lockers at ground level, while winged creatures were using lockers high above. The top of the dome must have been at least five hundred feet high. That's even taller than the Great Pyramids of Egypt! (I learned that listening in on King Khufu's class.)

In the middle of the room was a hundred-foot-tall statue of a fearsome-looking monster. It had the body of a gorilla, the legs of a raptor, and the tusked head of a wild boar. The body was covered in shining armor, but instead of holding up a sword, his right gorilla hand held up a scroll and his left hand grasped a feather quill. Instead of wearing a helmet, he sported a professor's cap.

"Who is that?" asked Charles.

"That is our beloved founder of Scream Academy, Garzok Grubshanks."

Charles walked by the statue. Garzok's name was chiseled into the stone pedestal. Underneath, a date was inscribed: JANUARY 1313—the year Scream Academy opened. Below that was Garzok's most famous quote: "Fear is the net that ensnares the mind."

That quote is pretty good, but Garzok has lots of good ones. My personal favorite is his advice to students trying to survive Scream Academy: "Be judicious or be delicious." Words to live by.

As the Scary School kids continued the tour, they were overwhelmed by all the monsters that filled the

room. On the ground were legions of troll kids. At Scary School there were only a few, but here they were one of the most common creatures. They had gray rhinolike skin with knobby heads, and they lumbered through the hall to their lockers, knocking smaller monsters out of the way. Rustling between them were the ogre kids with green skin. They would normally look pretty scary, but they appeared wimpy next to the big troll kids. The ogres are known to be very feisty, to make up for being smaller.

All seemed peaceful, but everything changed when one of the trolls stepped on an ogre's foot. Enraged, the ogre challenged the troll to a duel. They each walked back ten paces, faced each other, then charged. They clonked heads with a *thunk*, sounding like a home run baseball echoing through the chamber. Stumbling around dizzily, each tried to keep their balance, for whoever fell first would be the loser.

After a few moments, the troll fell over. The ogre was hoisted on the shoulders of his ogre friends and paraded around the room.

The parade stopped as soon as the ogres and trolls noticed the Scary School kids. Everyone became still, and you could feel the joyous mood of the room shift.

"Hey! What are human kids doing here?" the

winning ogre asked Principal Meltington.

Meltington answered, "If you guys would stop bashing your skulls, perhaps you'd remember the daily announcements. These are the human exchange students who will be visiting us for the week."

"But this is a school for monsters!" the losing troll roared, pushing the ogre out of the way while rubbing a bump on his head. "No humans allowed. Right, guys?"

The ogres and trolls roared in agreement.

"Wrong!" Meltington bellowed, hushing them up. "The great Garzok Grubshanks never said that humans were not allowed to learn here. He said only that it is a school where the ferocious could come to use their brains as well as their claws. I have chosen these humans because they're as ferocious as any of you. Show them, kids."

The six kids bared their teeth and growled at the monster kids.

The monster kids broke out into laughter.

"Har-har!" laughed the troll. "If even one human survives until lunch, I be very surprised. Come on, trolls."

The trolls marched off, and the ogres continued their celebratory parade. On his way out, the troll who had lost the duel bashed his head against the wall in anger. The force caused one of the lockers on the ceiling to come loose and fall straight toward his head.

Lattie was closest to the troll. She dove forward and pushed him out of the way at the last second. The locker left a huge hole in the floor. The troll grumbled, "Human saved my life? Ugh. Never will I hear the end of this." Then he stomped off without even saying thank you.

In the midst of the celebration, a group of green-skinned witch girls swooped over the scene riding on brooms. One of the witch girls pointed her wand at the ground and sprayed oil onto the floor. The ogres on parade slipped on top of one another. Cackling with delight, the witch girls zipped through an open window in the dome ceiling.

"Is this a normal day?" Wendy asked Principal Meltington.

"Oh, no. This isn't normal at all," he replied. "Usually, there are much crazier things going on."

A whole assortment of flying creatures entered the grand hall after the witches. There were gargoyles, pixies, fairies, dragons, flying monkeys, and flying fish! (The flying fish seemed to be snacks for the gargoyles and dragons, though.) On the ground were yetis, werewolves, orcs, and so many mixed-up monsters, I could hardly tell them apart.

Principal Meltington turned to the kids. "This is Garzok Hall, where everyone starts their day. You six can use lockers 310 through 320. Those are on the third level of lockers, so it's up to you to find a way up. Oh, and I'd suggest not opening an odd-numbered locker unless you want to spend the next several days trapped in a small space next to a goblin."

The kids knew how annoying the goblins of Goblin Hill were and shuddered at the thought.

The morning bell rang, which sounded like the bells of doom: *DONG! DONG! DONG!* Principal Meltington led the six to their first class, entering through one of seven dark corridors. Each corridor led to a different cave where the cave-dwelling teachers preferred to teach their classes. A skull and crossbones was mounted on the archway of the first corridor. The skull muttered, "Enter and ye shall never come out again!"

Principal Meltington chuckled and shook his head. "Don't mind him," he said. "He's almost never right."

The hallway was dark and ominous, lit only by flickering candles perched inside skull-shaped candleholders on the walls. Paintings of famous ghouls

hung everywhere. Their eyes followed passersby. One of the paintings howled at Jason, and he jumped in fright. The painted ghoul laughed so hard, it fell right out of the frame.

Trails of creepy bugs crawled along the ceiling. A giant roach fell on Wendy's shoulder and she shrieked. But no one noticed because there was a constant chorus of yelps from all the students in the hallway, as if the school were purposefully trying to compose its own symphony of screams.

The six kids entered a cave, brushing the roaches, centipedes, and beetles off their shoulders. Lattie did not brush away the bugs because Millie was having a blast making new friends.

"Welcome to your first class," said Principal Meltington. "Each of the seven corridors of the main hall leads to a different cave, where we hold our various classes. Tomorrow, you'll go down Corridor Two and so forth."

The rest of the monster students in the class were already seated on flat, heated rocks that kept them warm. Pointy icicles hung from the ceiling.

At Scary School, it was smart to avoid sitting next to a scary kid like Peter the Wolf who might bite you, but here at Scream Academy, there was no avoiding it.

In each seat there was a monster with sharp fangs or hooked claws or big muscles or stinky breath.

The Scary School students tried to find seats, but the monster students all growled whenever they tried to sit next to them. Eventually, they decided to play it safe and just stand in the back.

Then the slushy sound of footsteps in the snow was heard.

"Ah, your teacher has arrived," said Meltington. "And just in time, 'cause I'm starting to melt. Good luck!" Meltington vanished into a blizzard, leaving the exchange students all alone with the rest of the monster students and whatever in the world their teacher was.

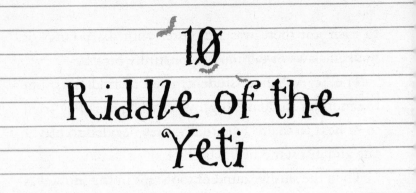

10
Riddle of the Yeti

runch. Crunch. Crunch.

Something was approaching from the dark depths of the cavern. The stomach-turning sound of bones being crushed echoed through the icy walls of the cave.

Petunia noticed that one of the students, an abominable snowkid who looked like a small version of Principal Meltington, was shaking with nerves. "Why are you afraid? Don't you know the teacher?" she asked him.

The snowkid turned to her and said, "No. It's our first class with him. He's been hibernating. But the stories we've heard about him . . . well . . . not everyone makes it out alive on the first day."

Petunia gulped, then glanced up at the pointy icicles that looked like they could fall at any moment. "Well, in case we don't survive, it was nice meeting you. My name is Petunia."

"Snowdy, Petunia. I'm Hubert. If you don't mind my asking, what are you?"

"She's a weirdo!" blurted a witch girl with green skin.

"Excuse me?" said Petunia, turning toward the witch.

"You heard me. Look at you! Who's ever seen a purple girl before? Gross!"

"What are you talking about?" said Petunia. "*You* have green skin."

"That's because I'm normal. All the most popular girls are green, and the rest are green with envy." She popped a small piece of chocolate in the shape of a human into her mouth and chomped down to emphasize her point.

The other witch girls shot sparks out of their wands at the same time, which is like a high five for witches.

"Be careful of her," whispered Hubert. "That's Ezelba, the meanest girl in school."

Petunia lowered her head and sighed. She thought things might be different here, but school was still school.

Jason jumped in and said, "Hey! I remember you!" pointing to Hubert the Snowkid. "You played ice hockey against us in last year's Ghoul Games."

"Snowdy!" Hubert replied. "I remember you, too! You were the best goalie I ever played against. Will you play on my team while you're here?"

"Sure!" Jason replied.

The happy reunion was broken up when a ten-foot-tall ivory-furred Sasquatch with thick twisting horns on its head entered the room.

"Ughhhh" moaned the creature. "I've had a very long hibernation, but it still feels like I've woken up at the crack of dawn. I'm in a *very* bad mood and I'm *very* hungry. If you make any loud noises, I might not be able to control my appetite."

The teacher noticed the Scary School kids standing at the back of the classroom. "Why are there humans in my cave? Are you my lunch?"

"Hello," said Wendy Crumkin, her voice a bit shaky from fright. "We're exchange students from Scary School."

Ezella

"Congratulations on knowing what you are, but I am not the least bit impressed. The question is, do you know what I am?"

"Yes," replied Wendy Crumkin. "You're a yeti."

"Ahh. Perhaps human brains are larger than a pebble after all. But do you know my name?"

"Umm . . . no," said Wendy.

"That's unfortunate," said the yeti. "Because nobody leaves here alive unless they know my name."

The students looked at one another nervously.

"So, do any of you pea-brains know my name?"

Nobody raised a hand.

"Most unfortunate indeed. But since I'm feeling in a slightly better mood seeing fresh human meat before me, I'm going to give you the opportunity to guess my name and save your skins."

The students exhaled a big sigh of relief.

"Who can tell me about the riddle of the Sphinx?"

Charles Nukid raised his hand. He knew all about the Sphinx from his lessons with King Khufu. The yeti called on him. "The Sphinx was an ancient monster with the body of a lion and the face of a woman that guarded the city of Thebes. To get past her you had to answer her riddle, but if you could not answer correctly, she would eat you."

"That's correct!" said the yeti. "In this class we will cover the ancient monsters, such as the Sphinx, many of which liked to tease their prey by asking them perplexing riddles. In honor of the Sphinx, let us begin this class with a riddle. Answer correctly, and you will live. Answer incorrectly, and well . . . they don't call this the scariest school in the world for nothing. Are you ready for your hint?"

The students got out their pencils and paper. The yeti cleared his throat, filling the room with his rotten breath.

You all can roar, you all can maim.
But can you guess this yeti's name?
It's said the same in Greek and Spanish.
Speak my name and I will vanish."

The students gathered into groups to discuss the hint. The Scary School kids huddled together and looked to Charles for the answer.

"So, what's the answer?" said Fred. "King Khufu must have taught it to you."

"Not this one," said Charles. "I have no clue."

"Do you know, Wendy?" asked Jason.

Wendy replied, "Riddles are meant to be unraveled. Let's break it down. 'It's said the same in Greek and Spanish. Speak my name and I will vanish.'"

Yeti Professor

Petunia noted, "The key to a riddle is to figure out the double meaning. What sort of thing will vanish when you say its name?"

"And it has to be a word that's the same in Greek and Spanish," Wendy added.

"I don't know Greek or Spanish!" said Fred, stomping his feet and brandishing his sharp nails. "Let's just take down the yeti."

"Bad idea," said Petunia. "Yetis have been hunted for years. If this one's still alive, it's for a reason."

The abominable snowkids joined the Scary School group. "Snowdy, folks! Do you have it figured out?" inquired Hubert.

"No. Do you?" asked Jason.

"Nope."

Then a group of trolls proudly stomped up to the yeti.

"We know answer," said the lead troll with confidence. "Since this is Scream Academy, your name must be a scream."

The group of trolls began screaming so loudly everyone had to cover their ears. The sound waves shook the room so hard the icicles on the ceiling started cracking.

Pointy icicles fell all over the room as if it were raining deadly daggers. Lattie grabbed Charles by the collar and yanked him out of the way of an icicle that would have plunged straight through his egg-shaped head. All over the room, the kids were diving and rolling, but the trolls wouldn't stop screaming!

Eventually the trolls ran out of breath and smiled at the teacher, thinking they were the smartest kids in class.

The yeti responded, "That was . . . incorrect. And you've put me in a very bad mood once again." He reared back to pounce on the troll, but at that moment, an icicle snapped off and plunged straight into the troll's neck. The troll dropped dead.

"Great snowballs! Hurry!" said Hubert to his friends.

Hubert rushed over and quickly covered the troll with snow until he looked like a dead snowman. Then he placed two buttons on his face for eyes and a carrot for his nose, and intoned, "Snowmanicus vivaculous!" The troll-snowman rose from the ground, back to life as a snow monster!

"Argh . . . thanks!" said the newly minted snow monster with a growl. "I don't feel nearly as dead as before."

Charles and Lattie found a quiet corner where they could brainstorm.

"I can't think over their yapping," said Charles to Lattie.

Lattie replied, "The loudest in the room is often the weakest."

"Good point." Charles was trying hard to think, but the only thing popping into his head was Penny. He tried to shoo the image of her away so he could concentrate, but she kept coming back, so he decided to go with it. "I wonder what Penny would say?" he said to himself. "I know exactly what she'd say. Nothing." He paused for a moment. "Nothing? Wait a second. Nothing . . . *That's it!*"

Charles grabbed Lattie's hand and ran up to the group.

"Guys!" exclaimed Charles. "Follow me. And don't make a peep."

The Scary School kids followed Charles. They stood before the yeti, looking him in the eye. All six remained perfectly quiet.

"Well?" said the yeti. "Aren't you going to take a guess, or have you given up and are offering yourselves to be my brunch?"

Charles held his finger to his lips, instructing the others not to make a sound.

After a few more moments, the yeti's demeanor shifted, growing angry. "Grrrr! What's my name? Guess my name!"

The six remained quiet.

"Answer me!" growled the yeti in desperation. When there was still no response from the students, the yeti calmed down instantly and smiled broadly.

"Well done. The humans are correct. They have just saved all your lives. You may take your seats and we will begin class.

The monsters cheered, not really sure what just happened, but appreciating the result. They stood up from their seats and offered them to the Scary School kids as a thank-you.

"How did you know to do that?" Petunia asked Charles, as they took their seats.

"Because the answer was Silence. Speak its name, and it vanishes."

"Of course! Silence is the same in Greek and

Spanish," Wendy added. "Not to mention every other language."

"Ohhh," said the rest of the students. Most of the monsters still did not get it. If *you* get it, you have a super-brain.

The rest of the class went fantastically well. Charles in particular had a wonderful time learning about ancient monsters he had never heard of, from a real expert on the subject. His favorites were the Elder Dragons—the oldest, fiercest dragons ever born. Lattie was taking very intense notes as the yeti lectured about them. The Elder Dragons seemed like they must have been the scariest monsters that ever existed. Thankfully, they were all long dead, so they couldn't possibly be the scary monsters alluded to in the prophecy, but Charles had a sinking feeling in his stomach the moment that idea popped into his head.

After leaving the snowy cave at the end of class, Charles heard a faint squeak behind him. He turned and saw Millie the Millipede on the mountainside, struggling in the snow. She must have fallen out of Lattie's backpack.

Charles made a quick dash to retrieve the millipede for his friend, but when he bent down to pick her up, the snow gave way beneath his feet. In a blink, he was plummeting down an icy chasm toward certain death.

Why does this keep happening to me? Charles thought, remembering the time he fell off Dr. Dragonbreath into Monster Forest.

Lattie heard the fleeting yelp of Charles the moment he fell, but by the time she turned, Charles was gone. She ran as fast as she could, following Charles's tracks in the snow.

The tracks ended at a small hole that opened into a deep dark chasm. Lattie noticed the innumerable footprints of Millie, and it dawned on her that Charles had fallen in an effort to retrieve her pet. How did I not notice? Some ninja I am, she thought.

Determined to make up for her mistake, Lattie made a desperate attempt to dive into the fissure, but the opening was suddenly plugged by a blast of snow from Principal Meltington, who had returned to guide them to their next class. Meltington pulled Lattie away from the chasm with his sharp, branchy hands.

"Your friend was a victim of bad luck," he spoke. "The chasm drops thousands of feet. I will not lose another one of you today."

"Where's Charles?" Petunia asked Lattie.

Lattie took a deep breath and buried her feelings, for a ninja is never ruled by her emotions. She said stiffly, "Charles is no more."

The kids gathered into a group hug and hoped that Charles might be reborn in some way and not lost forever.

Principal Meltington thought their hugging was very strange. "I wouldn't do that if I were you. The heat might make you stick to each other like a tongue on a flagpole."

The five remaining kids kept hugging.

11

The Creature in the Ice

Seconds after Charles had fallen, his panic passed and he regained his wits. He was falling down a narrow icy crevasse. There was a slick wall of ice in front of his face and behind him. He looked down and saw a bed of sharp rocks about five thousand feet below. Knowing the rate of descent of a falling body is about one hundred and seventy-six feet per second, Charles calculated that he had about twenty-five seconds to think of a solution before he splattered.

Thinking fast, he took inventory of what he had

that might be helpful. He had the millipede in his left hand. Probably useless. He had his backpack on his back. If it had a parachute inside, that would be great, but all it contained were a few books and his Guitar Legend guitar.

Wait a second. The guitar. That just might work, thought Charles.

In midair, Charles pulled the guitar out of his backpack. The head was shaped like a lightning bolt, giving it a nice sharp edge. Perfect.

Deadly impact appeared to be just seconds away. Charles slid the guitar below his feet and jammed the sharp edge into the ice wall. It dug in nicely, slowing him down, but Charles was still falling, and now ice chips were flying into his face.

With the head of the guitar digging into the wall, Charles carefully pressed the neck into the other wall. The guitar became a wedge, bringing Charles to a grinding halt a split second before the ice wall ended, opening into a colossal cavern with at least another two hundred feet to the rocky floor.

"Phew," said Charles, dangling his legs off the side of the guitar. Millie crawled onto Charles's shoulder and gave him a sticky kiss on the cheek for saving her life.

One big problem was solved, but now an even

tougher problem remained.

How to get out.

Charles cried, "Hello!" but his voice bounced back as a sharp echo, with no response. He realized he was on his own. He looked more closely at the ice wall in front of him and gasped in shock.

Charles was staring at one of the strangest creatures he had ever seen, frozen in the ice right in front of him. It had the body of an old man wearing a long gray robe, but it had the head of a swordfish and a dorsal fin on its back. Charles pressed his nose against the transparent ice to get a better look at it. That's when it did something that nearly caused Charles to stumble off the guitar to his death.

It blinked.

Charles regained his balance and pounded on the ice. "Hey! Are you alive?"

The creature was unable to speak, but it moved

106

its eyes down and to the left, where its finger was pointing at a stick in the ice wall.

"You want the stick?" Charles asked.

The creature blinked, and Charles assumed that meant yes. Charles reached out as far as he could and dislodged the stick with his fingertips. The creature blinked with excitement.

"Millie," said Charles to the millipede on his shoulder, "do you think you can drill a small hole to its hand?"

Millie nodded. She went to work chomping on the ice wall, creating a thin tube toward the creature's frozen hand. Then Charles slipped the stick through, and it slid into the creature's outstretched palm. The creature closed its eyes . . . and vanished . . . only to reappear a moment later, standing next to Charles on the guitar. Before Charles could object, it had grabbed hold of him and leaped off the guitar.

Charles screamed as he and the creature plummeted downward, but then the creature raised the stick above its head and a parachute ejected from the tip. They floated down slowly into an icy cavern, landing on a pile of bones that were clearly the remains of the not-so-lucky others who had fallen over the years.

The parachute sucked itself back into the stick.

"Wow," said Charles. "Is that a magic wand?"

Rather than answering, the creature waved the stick, and Charles's guitar zoomed down the chasm on its own and buried itself inside his backpack.

"I'll take that as a yes," Charles said.

The creature shot a blast of fire from its wand, and a section of the icy cavern wall melted away, revealing an inner sanctum.

"Welcome to my inner sanctum," said the creature in a friendly, old man's voice that threw Charles for a major loop.

"Whoa. You can talk?"

"Of course I can talk! Have you ever met a fizard that *couldn't*? I just haven't spoken in a very long time. It took me a moment to remember how. Follow me."

The sanctum smelled like fish and mildew. In the middle of the room was a crystal ball on a small round table. There were bookcases filled with ornately bound books—the kind that hold ancient secrets. On the walls hung a collection of antique swords as well as old paintings of wizards performing feats of magic. One of them showed a soccer team with dragonfly wings.

But the weirdest thing was a huge fish tank that was just about overflowing with fish. The robed creature jumped into the fish tank, caught a fish in its mouth,

Marlin

then jumped back out, swallowing the fish down in one gulp.

"Ahhh. Now I feel better. Tell me, boy," said the creature. "What year is it?"

Charles told him what year it was, and the creature fell to the floor.

"My goodness. Could it have been that long? You see, when you're a fizard, you move backward through time. It's very hard to keep track. But it seems I've been stuck in that ice wall for more than two hundred years."

Charles had a very confused look on his face.

"Oh, excuse me, I forgot we fizards aren't very common in this time period. Two hundred years in the future, we're all over the place."

"If you don't mind my asking, who are you?"

"Oh, pardon me. My name is Marlin. I'm a fizard. Half fish. Half wizard."

"You must be the only fizard alive, 'cause I've never heard of one, and I've studied all the strange creatures."

"Strange is a relative term, young man. Two hundred years from now, you will look strange yourself. But I probably shouldn't say things like that. Revealing the future can cause *major* mishaps."

"I understand. My name is—"

"You don't have to say your name. I know exactly who you are. Everyone in the future knows your face. There's even a statue of you right up there on the surface."

"Oh yeah? Then who am I?"

"You're Charles Nukid, the famous would-be dragon slayer. You try to save Scream Academy from the Elder Dragon but get killed in the process."

Charles had a horrified look on his face.

"Oops. I probably shouldn't have said that," said Marlin.

"Wait a minute," said Charles. "Are you talking about the prophecy that says a human child will battle the scariest monster ever?"

"Well, I'd better be talking about it. I'm the one who made it! But it's not really a 'prophecy' because I saw everything happen with my own fish eyes in the future. I reported what I saw to my fizard brother who's currently living hundreds of years ago. I told him to let everyone know that a human named Charles Nukid would have to fight the scariest Elder Dragon of all time. And that it would be signaled by a catastrophic storm. Did you not get the full message?"

"The prophecy only says that a human kid will have to fight the scariest monster ever."

"Oh. Well, prophecies are like a game of telephone. They tend to get muddled over the generations. But this one actually held up pretty well!"

Charles was feeling sick. "So, it's true then. I'm going to have to fight an Elder Dragon."

The fizard shrugged. "Well . . . now it's getting complicated. Since I revealed your future to you, you might be able to avoid it and create a new future for yourself. But if it was fated that I tell you your future, there's still no way to escape your grisly doom. I'd give you a fifty-fifty chance."

Well, a fifty-fifty chance is better than no chance, Charles figured.

Charles walked over to the crystal ball on the round table. "Does this thing work?" he asked. Charles was hoping to catch a glimpse of his future to see if Marlin was telling the truth. Charles peered into the crystal ball, but no images revealed themselves.

Marlin started laughing. "Crystal balls are a bunch of baloney! Nobody believes you're a wizard unless you have one, though."

Marlin whipped out a suitcase and began throwing all his belongings into it—robes, potion bottles, pointy hats, scarves to wrap around his sword nose, and finally the crystal ball.

"Why are you packing?" Charles asked.

"I was trapped in ice for two hundred years! I deserve a vacation. I'm thinking the nice warm waters of the Bahamas. The mahimahis are so delicious there."

Charles ran over and slammed Marlin's suitcase shut. "Wait! You can't leave without telling me more about this dragon. If I have to fight one, I need to know what I should be studying."

Marlin shrugged. "I suppose that's fair enough. Tell me, what do you know about Elder Dragons?"

"I know that there are four Elder Dragons. The Mountain Dragon, the Sea Dragon, the Sky Dragon, and the Ice Dragon. Silence the Yeti was just telling us about them."

"Ah, very good. But did he inform you how one slays an Elder Dragon?"

"No."

"It's no easy task, for they are the size of a mountain! Dragons never stop growing, you see. The young ones are much smaller."

"Like my teacher Dr. Dragonbreath!"

"Yes! Dragonbreath! In my time he's as tall as a lighthouse. But that's *nothing* compared to an Elder Dragon! And the only way to kill one is to jab it with a sword in its most vulnerable place. Its nose."

Marlin made a slashing movement with his sword nose, which Charles had to dodge.

"Now that I think about it," said Marlin, scratching his fish head, "giving you a fifty-fifty chance was very generous. Its nose would be hundreds of feet high! I'm changing my prediction. I'll give you a twenty percent chance of survival."

Charles sighed. "Okay. So I'll need a sword."

"Oh, but not just any sword. If you jab its nose with a regular sword, you'll just make it sneeze. For each dragon, there exists only one sword that can defeat it. For the Mountain Dragon, you must use the Sword of Gold. For the Sea Dragon, the Sword of Salt. For the Sky Dragon, the Sword of Silver. And for the Ice Dragon, the Sword of Fire.

As he named each sword, Marlin swiftly whipped his sword nose. Charles dove out of the way and grabbed one of the antique fencing swords on the wall. He was able to deflect Marlin's next nose strikes.

"Careful!" said Charles. "I don't want to chop off your nose!"

"Go ahead and try! This is your first sword-fighting lesson. *En garde!*"

Marlin continued lunging at Charles with his sword nose, and after a few minutes, Charles became

astonishingly deft with the sword, blocking Marlin's attacks and countering with his own.

"Well done!" exclaimed Marlin. "Your swordsmanship makes you a natural dragon slayer! Then again, the evidence in my time proves otherwise. Then again, perhaps this fencing lesson has changed your future. Then again, maybe it's changed nothing."

Charles scratched his head, more confused than ever. "So, since we're in the ice realm, I'm guessing I'll have to fight the Ice Dragon."

"That's a detail of the future I probably shouldn't reveal." He paused, then said, "But yes."

"That means I'll have to use the Sword of Fire. Where do I get it?"

"Fool! Nobody knows where the legendary swords are! In fact, now that I think about it, giving you a twenty percent chance of survival was extraordinarily generous of me. Since you don't have the Sword of Fire, I'm going to give you a three percent chance."

Charles shook his head, afraid to say another word that would decrease his odds further. He had never hoped someone was completely insane as much as he did right then.

"Say, can your wand zap me out of here?" Charles asked. "My friends are probably worried about me."

"Are you nuts? I can't teleport anywhere I can't see! What if we reappeared inside someone else's body and they exploded? Here's what I can do, though."

Marlin waved his wand and tapped Charles on the head with it. Charles immediately transformed into an adorable baby seal. He was still wearing the polka-dot tie around his seal neck, which made him even more adorable.

"Why did you turn me into a seal?" Charles asked, but it sounded like a seal bark.

"So you can get out of here!" Marlin replied gleefully in fluent Sealish.

The fizard placed his sword nose on the icy floor and drew a circle with the sharp tip. Then he kicked the round section of ice away to reveal the frigid ocean churning underneath.

"Bahamas, here I come!" Marlin proclaimed. Then he whipped off his robe, revealing a slick wetsuit on his old-man body. He dove into the water and swam away, carrying his luggage behind him.

Charles the Seal put his flipper in the water, but then Marlin popped his head out of the ice hole. "I forgot to mention one last thing," he said. "Watch out for sharks."

12

Sleeping with Spiders

While Charles the Seal was deciding whether to brave the shark-infested waters, I flew back to Scream Academy where the students were getting ready for dinner.

The Scary School kids followed the abominable snowkids into the dining hall after finishing their homework in the Screaming Library. It was kind of tough for the Scary School kids to do their homework there because, unlike the Scary School library, which is so quiet you can hear a pin drop (since Ms. T will eat anyone who makes a noise), the Scream Academy library was the exact opposite. The library is haunted by so many poltergeists throwing books off the shelves, moving chairs around, and crashing through windows, that the screaming from the students is all but continuous.

The Scream Academy Dining Hall was a sight to behold. The wide variety of monsters each had different dining needs that had to be met. To the right was an arena where the most ferocious monsters who liked to hunt for food were chasing around wild game. After catching their dinner, they feasted on it raw. Gross!

In the middle of the hall, other monsters were roasting great beasts on spits over a roaring fire, which was surrounded by stone tables. There was no silverware or napkins anywhere. The monsters would simply wipe the juices with their furry arms and then lick their own fur clean like it was a second meal.

For the more civilized students there was a salad bar. Not too exciting, but there were bowls of newts, worms, and maggots to use as toppings. The Scary School kids went straight for the salad bar and brought handfuls of vegetables to their table.

"I miss Sue the Amazing Octo-Chef," said Wendy to Petunia.

"Me, too. These vegetables aren't cooked well at all. Now I know why most other kids don't like them!"

Hubert arrived at the table with some of his snowkid friends and plopped a roasted leg of beast down in front of them.

"Snowdy, folks," said Hubert, taking a big bite off the drumstick in his hand. "Feast on!"

"Feast on!" answered Fred and Jason, diving into the leg of beast with full abandon. Petunia and Wendy retched at the boys' monstrous behavior.

"Here," said Hubert, handing the girls colorful snow cones. "I brought you these."

"Thanks!" said the girls, taking a bite of the delicious ice.

"Hey, where's Lattie?" asked Petunia.

The students looked around. Then Fred pointed up. "There she is!"

Lattie was sitting high above the scene on a tiny ledge. No one knew how she could have possibly gotten up there, but she seemed to be enjoying her own quiet time away from the madness, not eating a bite of food but simply adding some leaves and herbs into a cup of hot water to make tea.

That night, the students hunkered down for bed in the Dorm Cave. All around the huge space, there was nothing but bare, sharp rocks.

"Hey, where are our beds?" asked Fred. "I need to go to sleep so I can wake up."

"Yeah, we better not be sleeping on sharp rocks," added Jason.

"Relax, warmies," said Hubert. "Your beds are here. They haven't been made yet."

"I don't see any beds that need to be made," Wendy asserted.

"No, not *made* like that. As in built!" The Scary School kids scratched their heads in confusion, but their dilemma was answered the next moment when hundreds of spiders the size of cars dropped down from the ceiling, suspended by webs from their spinnerets.

The spiders wove out of their own silk kid-sized hammocks suspended fifty feet in the air. None of the

Scary School kids liked the idea of sleeping in a web that a giant spider had made for them, but they didn't seem to have any choice.

Silence the Yeti stood beneath the web-hammocks and handed each kid a blanket. Once the blanket was received, he threw each student high into the air, and each landed softly in their hammock, placing the blanket underneath so as not to stick to the web.

After the Scary School kids saw how it worked, they decided it looked like a lot of fun. They eagerly took their turns flying into the air and landing in their sticky hammocks.

As the Scary School kids lay down to sleep, the thought of losing Charles finally hit them. They had held out hope that he would have shown up by now, as he always seemed to survive the direst circumstances. They had at least hoped he would have returned as a ghost or a zombie.

Most of the troll and ogre kids fell asleep immediately and started snoring like buzz saws. The Scary School kids didn't mind, though, because it gave them a chance to talk without disturbing the others.

Wendy said, "I remember when Charles taught us all how to catch our desserts on Halloween."

Petunia said, "I remember when he came flying

back with Princess Zogette after falling into Monster Forest. We thought he was a goner for sure that time, but he came back."

As usual, Lattie kept quiet in her hammock, but she was feeling sadder than she'd ever felt. On the same day, she had lost her only two friends in the world—Charles and Millie. Ninjas are not supposed to ever feel emotion, but that night she cried for the first time in her memory.

13

Rory, the Monster Who Couldn't Roar

While the students were fast asleep in the spider-web beds, it occurred to me that the students at Scary School could be having their own problems with the exchange students from Scream Academy. I decided to go back to make sure none of my friends had been eaten.

I hitched a ride on a polter-bear (us ghosts can interact with one another) and made it all the way

Rory

back to Scary School in time for recess. It looked like all my friends were still alive, so I used the time to get to know the exchange students.

Since arriving from Scream Academy, the three exchange monsters were trying their best to fit in at such a different school. One was a Cyclops named Cy Clops. Super convenient! Another was an invisible kid named Scotty. Nobody saw him the entire week. The third was a nine-year-old monster named Rory.

During recess, Rory was sitting all alone by the alligators at the bottom of Scary Slide, throwing them little fish snacks. He was hoping someone would join him, but he was very scary-looking, and everyone was afraid to come near him.

Being near those man-eating alligators didn't help.

At Scream Academy, Rory was considered one of the least scary-looking kids, but here at Scary School, where scary kids were more rare, he looked absolutely terrifying. He was the size of a human adult (already pretty scary), shaped like an apple, and covered in blue fur. He had only one part to his body, so he looked kind of like a giant head. His long arms jutted out where his ears should be and went all the way to the ground. He had short, stubby legs that were all but useless. His mouth took up half of his body, and his teeth looked like unpeeled bananas. Plus he had eyeballs the size of baseballs and a furry unibrow that stretched across his forehead.

Sitting by those gators, Rory was feeling more and more homesick with each fish he threw in their mouths. He wished over and over that he could just go back home.

That's when he heard a voice from behind him.

"Hey, you!"

Standing there were Johnny the Sasquatch, Peter the Wolf, and Ramon the Zombie—probably the three coolest kids at Scary School. Next to them was one of the exchange students from Scream Academy, Cy Clops the kid Cyclops, who held a baseball bat over his shoulder.

"Hello," said Rory, in a voice that sounded like a tuba because his mouth was so big.

Johnny remarked, "Cy Clops here says your name is Rory. Is that true?"

"It true."

"You wanna play baseball with us? We need another player."

"Baseball? I can no play. Helmet no fit my head."

"That's too bad. Cy is the bes—" Ramon's tongue fell out of his mouth, and he quickly picked it up and reattached it. "Sorry. My tongue is loose today. We thought you might be as good as Cy. He's the best hitter we've played with."

"That's because I always keep my eye on the ball," said Cy.

"I'm no good," said Rory.

"Say," said Ramon the Zombie, "you have the biggest head I've ever seen. If your brain is just as big, could I pleeease have just a small bite? You wouldn't miss it."

"Uhhh . . . no, thank you. I think I need every piece of my brain."

"Smart move," said Peter the Wolf. "The last kid who let Ramon try his brain forgot all his multiplication tables and thought his teacher was his mom. But since you can't play baseball, how about another game?"

"What kind of game?"

"With a name like Rory, you must have the scariest roar ever. How this game works is each of us will go around the school yard and roar as loudly as we can. Whoever can scare the most kids off the playground wins."

"Okay, I can try that one."

Johnny, Ramon, Peter, Cy, and Rory strolled over to the quicksand box, where a group of third graders was building quicksand castles. Johnny let out his scariest Sasquatch roar, and a bunch of kids scattered. Except for one kid who sank into the quicksand and popped up in the middle of Scary Forest, where survival was highly unlikely. Life lesson, kids. Don't play in quicksand.

Johnny did a quick count. "I scared eight kids right out of the box! All right!"

"Ahh! Eight such a small number!" said Rory. "Remember to use Monster Math and say eight million, or I might have heart attack."

Next, Peter the Wolf did his best werewolf howl at the monkey bars of doom. "Nine million kids got scared. I'm in the lead!"

Ramon the Zombie did his best zombie growl at the possessed merry-go-round, but only five kids got scared. "Kids just aren't as afraid of zombies as they used to be," grumbled Ramon.

Cy Clops tried his cyclopsian growl at the Pit of Scarflakk, and twelve kids ran away screaming. "Ha-ha! Twelve billion! Beat that!"

Rory stomped over to the slayground area. There were at least fifty kids running across the bridges and dodging the swinging ax blade. If he let out a good roar, he could totally smash the others for the win. The four friends grinned in anticipation.

Rory sucked in a deep breath, reared back, and tried to roar the loudest he ever had. But all that came out was a flimsy wheezing sound: *Hfffafafa. Hfffafafa.*

Oh no, not now, Rory thought.

Rory had a bad case of monster asthma, which always seemed to flare up at the worst possible moments. He reached into his backpack and pulled out an inhaler the size of a thermos. He took a deep puff on it and tried roaring one more time. It was even worse than before. *Pfffff! Pffffff!* Then he started coughing and fell over face-first onto the fire-ant hill. The ants were biting him all over his face, which was his entire body.

He rolled away, brushed himself off, and took two more big puffs on the inhaler, gasping for breath.

The four friends glared at him with severe disappointment.

"Well, that was a bummer," said Ramon.

"Let's go, guys," said Johnny. "He's not scary at all."

Rory took another big puff on his inhaler and felt like crying, but he held back, not wanting to be embarrassed any further. He couldn't believe he had had his big chance to make some friends and he blew it.

That's when Rory noticed a girl lying next to him who appeared to be dead. He nudged her, but she didn't move.

Uh oh, thought Rory. I hope I didn't accidentally squash her when I rolled over. He reached over to feel her neck for a pulse, but as soon as he touched her, Penny Possum leaped upward, which scared Rory half to death. Rory made a wheezy sound, spun around, and fell back on the ground (and yes, I'm a ghost poet and I know it).

Penny giggled on the inside. She had played dead
when she saw Rory next to her because he looked so
scary, but now he didn't seem very scary at all.

She helped Rory up and brushed a few remaining
red ants off his blue fur.

"Hoofah! Thank goodness you not dead," said
Rory. "My name Rory. What's your name?"

Penny was always ready for this question. She took
a penny out of her sweater pocket and held it up.

"Your name Penny?"

Penny nodded.

"I like your name. You no talk?"

Penny shook her head.

"That okay," said Rory. "I think humans and monsters make too much noise anyway."

Penny smiled. It felt good to have an exchange with someone. She wouldn't admit it to herself, but she missed having Charles around to not talk to.

"Well, since you no talk, I guess I go back to feeding gators. Nice meeting you. Hopefully you bring me good luck just like a penny."

Penny had seen what happened earlier when Rory tried to scare the kids on the playground. A brilliant idea came to her. As Rory turned to walk away, she grabbed him by the hand and pulled him over to the tetherball court. There, Frank (pronounced "Rachel") was playing a game of invisible tetherball with Mr. Grump. Unfortunately, the tetherball had broken free from its pole earlier in the week and was currently lurking around the school yard bopping unsuspecting kids on the head to show them how it felt.

Frank was very good with any game using invisible ropes and won her tetherball matches every time, even though there was no ball and no string. When she beat

Mr. Grump with one mighty pummel, she turned to the girls at the hopscotch courts and demanded, "All right, who's next?"

Everyone backed away in fear, not wanting to get lassoed by Frank's invisible ropes.

Next, Penny brought Rory to the benches under the poisonous apple tree. There, a group of fifth graders was reading a new story Steven Kingsley had just written. After surviving the monster attack last semester, he finally had the courage to start writing scary stories, and the kids loved reading them. They made Scary School seem not quite so scary by comparison. The kids huddled close as they read Steven's stories while he watched from a distance, enjoying their reactions.

Finally, Penny brought Rory to the shores of Scary Pool. A group of angry seventh graders was chasing Fritz for making them lose yet another basketball game. To evade them, Fritz jumped into the water, where he felt much more comfortable. "Come out of there!" the seventh graders yelled. "You can't stay in there forever!" A moment later, Fritz rose out of the pool riding on the neck of his friend Nessie the Loch Ness Monster. Nessie shot a stream of water out of her nostrils right at the seventh graders. They tumbled across the shore, then ran away screaming.

Rory turned to Penny and said, "Ohhh, I get why you show me this. You trying to teach me that there are lots of ways to be scary beside roaring."

Penny nodded vigorously.

"Hoofah! I never thought of that. Thank you!"

Later that day, Johnny, Ramon, Peter, and Cy were playing baseball during lunch period. Johnny pitched the ball to Cy, who took his eye off it for the first time, and it clonked him in the head. But Cy didn't even flinch because he was too distracted by what was coming toward him.

Three alligators were charging right at them. Standing on the middle gator's tail was Rory, holding on to three ropes tied to each gator's head as a harness.

Rory took a puff on his inhaler and commanded, "Full speed ahead!"

The chariot of alligators stormed across the baseball field, bellowing and snapping their jaws. Johnny, Ramon, Peter, and Cy shrieked and dove out of the way. Next, Rory turned the gators around and drove them across the school yard, clearing the terrified kids away from every single piece of playground equipment.

Johnny, Ramon, Peter, and Cy were so impressed that they stood up and cheered Rory's incredible feat.

Nobody had *ever* been scary enough to frighten all of the kids off the playground before. Even Penny was so scared that she played dead, but she enjoyed every second of it.

Once he was finished, Rory hopped off the gators, threw each one a fish, and gave them a pat on the head. When he turned around, the entire school was cheering for him.

Ramon said to Peter, "Let's make that guy an extra-extra-extra-large helmet so he can play baseball with us!"

The next day, all of the kids were begging Rory to come play games with them and teach them how to ride the gators. The kids took turns squeezing Rory's inhaler for him whenever he felt wheezy.

Just yesterday, Rory couldn't wait to go back home. Now he never wanted to leave.

14

Swimming with Sharks

Charles the Seal sat in the sanctum replaying Marlin's words in his head: "One last thing. Watch out for sharks." Charles had wanted to scream back, "If there are sharks, why did you turn me into a seal?" but Marlin had swum away. Swimming with sharks was still the last thing he wanted to do. So he spent a whole day trying to find another way out of the cave. There was none.

Since Marlin believed Charles was going to die fighting a dragon, in his fizard mind, there was no

need for Charles to worry about swimming through shark-infested waters. That didn't make Charles feel any better about it.

Before facing the icy ocean, he practiced seal swimming in Marlin's fish tank to get the feel for it, and the next morning, he took his chances and dove into the ocean with his backpack strapped to his flipper. Millie was stowed safely in the backpack's airtight pocket.

As soon as he entered the water, he scanned for sharks. Fortunately he didn't see any. He began swimming around, looking for an opening in the ice above, but couldn't find one. Then he saw a creature swimming toward him. It was another seal! Charles barked, "Do you know the way out?"

But all it barked back was, "What are you doing? Swim!" It quickly swam by, and

Charles turned to see that a school of blue sharks was swimming after it. Without a moment to think, Charles followed the seal, swimming as fast as he could. They soon met up with the rest of the seal's pod. All of them began swimming for their lives, but Charles was the least experienced and was lagging behind.

The sharks were right upon Charles, already nipping at his seal tail. He was running out of energy, and the weight of his backpack was a burden. He cursed himself for not leaving it behind.

The sharks caught up with him. Two of them swam next to him, one on each side, and lunged forward, jaws-first, for their strikes. But right before they could chomp down on his seal flesh, something caught on Charles's flipper and yanked him upward.

Charles rose quickly through the water and was pulled up through a circular hole in the ice. Silence the Yeti looked at Charles the Seal dangling on the end of his fishing hook and exclaimed, "Yummy! Breakfast!"

It was out of the frying pan into the fire.

15

The Witches' Brew

That morning at Scream Academy, the five Scary School kids walked down Corridor Two for the day's class. Charles had still not shown up, and his friends were very close to giving up hope, but they still held out a glimmer that Charles might be sitting in the classroom waiting for them when they got there.

Unlike the previous day's corridor that made the kids scream by freaking them out with falling insects and moving paintings, this hallway had a different method. The armor of past monster knights stood against the walls, holding monstrous swords and maces. It was quiet. Too quiet.

The Scary School kids decided to huddle together and walk as a unit. Jason and Fred were looking straight ahead when something moved. They immediately shouted, "Sword!"

All five kids ducked in the nick of time as a knight swung its broadsword over their heads. Then Wendy shouted, "Claw!" and all five took cover on the ground as a claw from above reached down but grabbed only air.

Then a monster walking in front of them screamed, "Waaaaah!" as it fell through a trapdoor that opened in the ground. It was now clear what this corridor was all about: booby traps. While the walkers were distracted by knights swinging their maces, trapdoors would open, walls would spin around, and claws would reach down to snatch you!

A scary moment occurred when a trapdoor opened right under Petunia's feet. But the Scary School kids were all holding on to one another's arms, and they were able to keep Petunia above ground so she didn't fall into the darkness.

The classroom door was dead ahead. It seemed like

more than half of the students who had entered the corridor were already gone. The Scary School kids were just steps away, thinking they had made it through the worst, but then a barrage of arrows shot out from the doorway straight toward them. The five closed their eyes, thinking it was all over, but when nothing happened, they realized that Lattie had caught the arrows in mid-flight using her lightning-quick ninja reflexes.

"Wow! Thanks, Lattie!" they all said.

Lattie snapped an arrow in half and said, "A single arrow is easily broken, but not five in a bundle."

When all five Scary School kids entered the classroom, they looked around for Charles, but he wasn't there. The monster students who had made it looked shocked when the human kids entered.

"Greetings, young ones," they heard from three voices speaking in unison.

The teacher was already there, but it wasn't just one teacher. There were three old witches with long gray hair and black robes. None of them had eyes.

"We are your teacher, Ms. Coven," said a witch with a shaky voice, holding what looked like an eyeball against her forehead.

"Give me the eye!" shrieked one of the other witches. "I want to look at them."

One of the witches grabbed the eyeball from the hand of the first witch and placed it against her forehead. "Ah yes, humans are adorable at this age, aren't they?"

"Adorable and delectable," said another witch, causing them to cackle in unison.

"Please take a seat. The brew is almost ready," said the witch holding the eye, offering them an aisle of empty seats.

"Hey!" grunted a furry brown monster with fangs jutting up from its lower jaw. "Yesterday there were six thousand human kids. I count only five million now." The kids did some quick Monster Math and deduced he meant five.

"One of our friends fell down a chasm yesterday," said Petunia as she took a seat in the front row.

The class erupted in laughter. A troll girl with pink pigtails on her lumpy gray head giggled, "Hardy-har-har! Dumb-dumb human. Can't avoid a chasm!"

"Mmmm . . . they look sooo delicious," said a spotted monster who drooled and licked its chops.

"I bet the purple girl tastes like grapes!" said a rotund ogre.

"Patience, students," said Ms. Coven. "There will be no eating of the exchange students. Unless, of course, we give you permission."

The Scary School kids gulped. The witches were slowly stirring the bubbling liquid in their cauldron and throwing in ingredients that ignited sparks.

Then vents opened in the ceiling. The sounds of screaming drew closer and closer until monsters started dropping through vents and into chairs at their desks. They were the same monsters who had fallen through the trapdoors and gotten snatched up by the claws in the corridor. It appeared the trapdoors were tunnels that led all the way back to the classroom. Now the Scary School kids were upset they didn't fall through. It seemed like a lot of fun!

"Now that we're all here," said Ms. Coven, "it's time to teach you how to make a potion that should be in every monster's arsenal. The potion of—whoops!"

The eye slipped out of the witch's hand and started rolling across the floor.

"My eye! Give me my eye!"

The witches started crawling along the floor with their hands out, desperately searching for the eye.

The monsters in the class were laughing. Whenever one of the witches got close to the eye, a monster kicked it across the room to one of their friends like a game of eyeball soccer keep-away!

"Where is our eye?" the witches continued pleading. "Why won't any of you give us back our eye?"

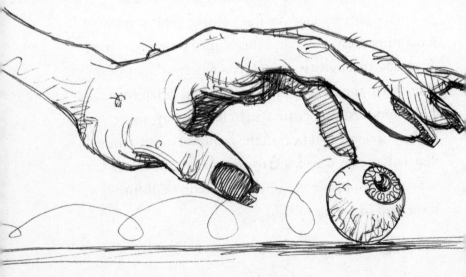

Eventually, the eyeball landed at the feet of Ezelba the Witch Girl. She was again eating a box of human-shaped chocolates and refusing to share with anyone else, but she stopped stuffing her face to pick up the eyeball. She put it in her backpack and zipped it shut.

"It's so dark!" moaned Ms. Coven. "Where's the eye? In a mouse hole?"

Ezelba put a finger to her lips, ordering the class to stay quiet. The monsters obeyed and told the teacher they couldn't find it.

"Fine," said Ms. Coven. "We will teach you without the eye. But if we find one of you is keeping it from us, you'll wish you were never born!"

The threat seemed to have no effect on Ezelba, who just smiled to herself and got wand fives from her friends.

Gathering back around the cauldron, the witches continued, "We're not going to even tell you what this potion does anymore. You'll have to find out on your own."

"Unless you give us back the eye!"

Ms. Coven went back to throwing items into the cauldron. "Take notes on the ingredients that go into the brew!" Ms. Coven had to feel and sniff each ingredient before throwing it in, which made everyone snicker.

Petunia was diligently taking notes when Wendy tapped her on the shoulder and handed her a note. Rolling her eyes, Wendy said, "The boys wanted me to give you this."

Petunia unfolded the note. It read: *Who do you like more? Jason or Fred? Circle one.*

Did she really *have* to pick one right then? Was that the rule of note passing? She turned around, and Jason and Fred were flexing their muscles.

Luckily, she didn't have to decide at that moment because the note flew out of her hand and floated across the room, landing on the desk of Ezelba.

"Rules of the class," said Ezelba the Witch Girl. "If someone passes a note, everyone gets to read it."

Ezelba read the note aloud and started cackling. "Those boys must be blind. How could they like someone purple? You look like you took a bath in prune juice!"

"Quiet!" Ms. Coven shouted. "You should be writing down the ingredients of the potion. Toe of tiger, feet of frog, nose of newt, and eye of hog. Speaking of eyes, has anyone found our eye yet?"

Nobody was paying attention to Ms. Coven. The class saw Petunia was getting upset and wouldn't let up. "Purple girl! Purple girl! We'll eat you, then we'll burp a girl!"

Petunia wanted to dig herself into a hole, but then Fred and Jason stood up on their desks.

"Enough!" Fred shouted. "If you have a problem with Petunia, you have a problem with us."

Then Jason pulled out his hockey stick from his backpack, and Fred pulled out his silver hammer. Jason tossed a hockey puck in the air and smacked it with his stick. The puck flew around the room, ricocheting off the walls and shattering jars of specimens. The students ducked out of the way. Then Fred raised his silver hammer and smashed his desk into a million pieces.

"What's going on?" Ms. Coven demanded. "We can't see what's happening! We have no eye!"

Wendy pulled out her Monster Math calculator and shouted, "Negative thirty-six!" The monsters in the class felt their blood curdle in fear at the horrifically small number.

With the students distracted, Lattie leaped out of her seat, did a triple somersault in the air, skipped over a troll's head, then landed on Ezelba's desk with the grace of a cat. She looked her right in the eyes and said, "Before dispensing your opinion, remember first if anyone asked you for it."

"O-okay," said Ezelba, shaking. "I won't tease her again. Just don't ninja me or something."

Petunia smiled, seeing that her classmates actually cared about her enough to stand up for her.

Lattie snatched the note out of Ezelba's hand, bounced off the ceiling, and dropped the paper in Petunia's lap, capping her maneuver with a spectacular backflip onto the rim of the cauldron, where she placed Ms. Coven's eye back in her hand. Like a sleight-of-hand artist, she must have sneakily snatched the eye back without anyone noticing! I gave her a standing ovation but no one could hear my ghost hands clapping.

"You found our eye! Thank you so much young . . . human? Well, perhaps we won't be feasting on you after all."

A zombie girl turned to the witch girl and said, "Hey, Ezelba, maybe we shouldn't mess with these human kids."

Suddenly, the door burst open and Silence the Yeti entered, carrying a young seal that was wearing a polka-dot tie.

"Ms. Coven," spoke Silence. "I wanted to make sure this seal wasn't one of your students before I ate him."

Ms. Coven examined the seal with her eye. "Nope. Never seen him. Eat away."

"Hurray!" said the yeti, getting ready to stuff Charles

the Seal into his gigantic mouth.

The seal barked, "I'm not a seal! I'm Charles Nukid. I got turned into a seal by a fizard!" At least that's what Charles thought he said, but all the class heard was the *bark! bark!* of seal calls. Charles couldn't believe he was about to meet his end by being eaten by a yeti. Talk about embarrassing.

The yeti was just about to chomp down on Charles's seal head when Petunia yelled, "Wait! That's not a seal. That's Charles Nukid!"

"Huh?" said the yeti, taking Charles out of his mouth.

"Look on his flipper!" On Charles's flipper was the backpack with the guitar sticking out. Then Millie the Millipede crawled up the guitar neck.

"Millie!" Lattie shrieked in a rare outburst of emotion. She leaped onto the yeti, and Millie crawled onto her shoulder, coughing up seawater and nuzzling her cheek.

"If this is your friend," said Ms. Coven, "a student transforming into an animal is the number one rule not to break! You may continue with your meal, Mr. Yeti."

Hearing that he was breaking the rules filled Charles with renewed vigor. If it was his time to die, by golly, he would die following the rules. He began thrashing and squirming in the yeti's hands. A slippery oil exuded from his seal skin, and he slid right through the yeti's grip, landing on the floor. Then he paddled his flippers and slid on his belly up and down the aisles as the angry yeti chased after him.

Lattie was still riding on the yeti's shoulders and covered its eyes. "You cannot hunt what you cannot see!" Lattie exclaimed. The yeti tripped over a desk and crashed down onto two other desks, smashing them to bits.

The class cheered, "Go seal! Go seal!" Even Ms. Coven cheered with them.

Ezelba pointed her wand at Charles, and he rose into the air. "There's one way to settle this," she said. "Abra vitulina!" There was a flash from her wand, and Charles transformed back into his human self, wearing the gray shorts, white dress shirt, and polka-dot tie.

The class erupted in laughter.

"Look at him," cackled Ezelba. "What kind of silly outfit is that?"

"Yeah, and he's as skinny as a toothpick!" laughed the troll girl.

"Let's call him Toothpick!" the zombie girl suggested.

"Toooothpick! Toooothpick!" the class mocked.

Charles sighed. Even halfway around the world, he couldn't escape that dreaded nickname.

"Don't call him Toothpick," said Ms. Coven. "Charles is a part of our class now." The class begrudgingly quieted down. "Besides," Ms. Coven added, "he has no chance of lasting long here. He has the skinniest noodle neck I've ever seen."

"Noodle-neck! Noodle-neck!" the class chanted.

Charles didn't like that nickname any better. His friends didn't care what his nickname was. They were so overjoyed that he was back they gave him high fives and patted him on the shoulder.

Class resumed with a few small changes. Silence the Yeti was passed out on the floor, so the students whose desks had been crushed by his fall were using his white fluffy back as their desk.

Finally, Ms. Coven finished her brew by chanting, "And the final step so you won't die, the wing set of a dragonfly."

She placed a dragonfly wing in the cauldron, and the potion dramatically changed color from sludgy black to bright green. Then she placed small black cauldrons on everyone's desks and ladled a scoop into each one.

"Since you've been paying such close attention," said Ms. Coven, "I'm sure you'll know exactly what to do with these."

Nobody had been paying close attention. Not even me.

The ogre took a small sip. He turned into a newt. A brown furry monster rubbed some on his hand. He turned into a toad.

Ms. Coven cackled, "Nobody is allowed to leave this class until you've used this potion properly."

That's when Charles had an idea. He remembered seeing the painting on Marlin's wall of a Scream Academy soccer team with dragonfly wings. Didn't Ms. Coven just add a dragonfly wing into her brew?

It was a long shot, but he decided to take a chance. After all, it couldn't be any worse than being a seal, right?

Charles took a spoonful and poured it down his back.

"Charles! What are you doing?" his friends shouted. But a second later, dragonfly wings sprouted from his shoulder blades and he started flying around the room.

"Whoo-hoo!" he cried. "This is awesome."

Soon everyone had copied him, and they were flying around the room. "Good job, Noodle-neck!" said

the troll girl. "We'll call you Charles Nukid from now on!"

The lunch bell rang, and Charles flew straight into the lunch hall. But the potion wore off unexpectedly, and he fell right into a big tub of noodles.

Lattie fell from up near the ceiling, but was caught in the arms of the same troll she had saved the first day at Scream Academy. "Now we even," said Tommy the Troll. It stomped away before Lattie could even express her gratitude. I guess some creatures have their own way of saying thank you.

Charles crawled out of the tub and was covered in noodles. All the monsters laughed.

His nickname went back to being Noodle-neck.

16

Lattie and the Trampoline

During lunch, everyone from Ms. Coven's class came and sat at the table with the Scary School kids. Even the abominable snowkids rushed over and fought with the other monsters over who would get to sit next to them.

Charles began telling the story of what happened after he fell in the chasm. He told them about how he survived the fall by using his guitar, how he freed Marlin the Fizard, and how he barely survived the shark chase in the ocean.

The monster kids were so enthralled that they didn't even touch the caribou carcass lying on the table.

Eventually he got to the part about how Marlin predicted that he was destined to battle the Ice Dragon. He chose not to mention that he was supposed to die doing so. That just didn't seem cool. But as soon as Charles said "Ice Dragon," a low, menacing growl could be heard at the table. It wasn't coming from any of the monsters. It was coming from Lattie.

It was a morning much like any other at the ninja monsterstery. The thick fog rolled through the mountain pass like a soft gray river, and the magnificent red temple sat atop the snowy mountain peak like a gleaming cherry on a mound of ice cream.

This was where Master Three Claws trained his monster pupils in the ninja arts. Only those deemed worthy were allowed to live and study at the temple, and the competition for admission was fiercer than a bearodactyl protecting its cubs. Unfortunately, the only students who ever applied were savage monsters, so Master Three Claws didn't usually get the most disciplined students, but he enjoyed the challenge of molding his ferocious disciples into focused thinkers and fearless masters.

Master Three Claws had a wrinkled face that looked something like a shar-pei dog, but with the long ears and whiskers of a lynx, and the chubby body of a teddy bear. He appeared incredibly appetizing to any monster that looked upon him, which was why self-defense was so important to him.

He was not called Three Claws because he had three claws. In fact, he had no claws. His paws were actually as puffy and harmless as a declawed kitten's. He was called Three Claws because of the three scars that ran diagonally across his wrinkled face, where a monster with three claws had once slashed him.

It was that encounter that made Three Claws realize that he would have to find other ways to defend himself against the vicious monsters that wanted to make a meal of him.

But, as I was saying, eleven years ago, on a morning much like any other, something extraordinary happened. Master Three Claws was supervising the monsters in their daily chores—preparing for a long day of training in combat and stealth—when there was a loud knock at the monsterstery door.

"Oh, goody!" said one of the monster students. "Breakfast is here!"

Master Three Claws bopped the monster on the

head with his staff and said, "The superior man does not, even for the space of one meal, act contrary to virtue."

Master Three Claws

The monster grumbled and continued mopping the floor.

Master Three Claws opened the temple doors to find a small basket sitting on the doorstep. In it, a human baby was wrapped in a blanket with the name LATTIE stitched into it.

The monsters immediately smelled the human flesh, dropped their mops, and ran to the entryway.

"Oh, master! You bring us a human baby for breakfast! What a gift!" A monster with long tusks made a lunge for the baby, but Master Three Claws snatched him by the tusks, twirled him over his head, and threw him across the room.

"This is not your breakfast," said Three Claws, "but it is certainly a gift."

That night, Lattie was asleep in the nursery that the frustrated monsters had been ordered to build. But the sweet smell of human meat was too much to resist, and three of them snuck in to have a midnight snack.

Using their ninja skills, they tiptoed into the nursery and were so quiet they didn't even wake the sleeping baby or stir Master Three Claws, who was sleeping nearby. They lifted the blanket and whispered: "I want the legs!" "I want the arms!" "I want the belly!"

The biggest monster reached down, drooling in

anticipation, but then felt something bite its finger. "Ouchies!" the monster shouted, seeing a baby millipede with huge fangs clamped onto its finger. The millipede swung herself onto the next monster and bit him on the ear, then bit the next monster on his snout.

Crying in pain from the millipede's potent poison, the monsters ran back to their rooms. Master Three Claws had noticed the baby millipede crawl into Lattie's basket when he first found it and knew that it and the child would be lifelong friends.

By the way, in case you're an animal expert, it's true that millipedes don't usually bite. They actually can't. But Millie is a millipede mixed with a rhinoceros beetle, which has one of the strongest bites in the animal kingdom. I guess that makes her more of a monster-pede!

Two years later, Lattie was already well into her ninja training. She learned to kick and chop before she could even walk. Her favorite food was sweet sugar cookies, and Master Three Claws was careful to give them to her only as a very special reward. This drove Lattie crazy. She was so tired of the rice and spinach she had to eat at almost every meal.

One day, she saw Master Three Claws place the box of cookies on the top shelf in the kitchen pantry.

Lattie tried all morning to jump up to reach them, but she didn't even come close. That made her so mad she stomped her foot on the floor until the floorboard beneath her broke apart, revealing a small, hidden crawl space filled with old rubber mats. They looked like they hadn't been used for hundreds of years.

That gave Lattie her very first brilliant idea.

She ran to her room, pulled out the springs from her bed and attached them to a rubber mat. In no time she had assembled a crude trampoline. It took some practice, but soon she was able to jump off the trampoline all the way to the top shelf, where she smartly removed just one sugar cookie from the box so Master Three Claws wouldn't notice. Then she hid the trampoline in the crawl space and replaced the floorboard.

It was a lot of work for one cookie, but when all you have to eat is rice and spinach and the occasional codfish, it's totally worth it.

One year later, Lattie went into the kitchen for her daily routine of swiping another sugar cookie, but she found that a whole new set of shelves had been built above the ones already there. The box of cookies was now placed even higher than before. It took weeks of jumping on the trampoline before Lattie was finally able to reach the cookies at the new height. The next day, the cookies were placed on a higher shelf, and it took more weeks of jumping to reach those ones. And so it went until a year had passed, and the cookies were on a shelf all the way at the ceiling, and there was no place higher for them to go.

Or so Lattie thought.

One morning, Lattie walked into the kitchen, and the box of cookies was gone. Oh no, Lattie thought. Master Three Claws has finally caught on to my trick.

Of course, Master Three Claws had caught on long ago, but four-year-old Lattie didn't realize that.

That day, a very angry Lattie entered the Combat Hall for her daily lessons in combat. The hall's ceilings were fifty feet high and the walls were a sheer polished stone. Hanging on the sides was a collection of swords and helmets and weaponry that would be the envy of the grandest ancient army. But the prized possession was a sword encased in glass marked THE SWORD OF GOLD.

That's when Lattie noticed that sitting on a small platform, right beneath the high ceiling of the hall, was the box of cookies. But it was so high up!

Master Three Claws appeared next to Lattie and asked, "Would you like a cookie?"

"Yes, master."

165

"Very well. You may take one."

"But the box is too high up."

"That never stopped you before, now did it?" Master Three Claws winked. It seemed like permission to use the trampoline, so she ran to the crawl space to pull it out, but came back empty-handed.

"The trampoline is gone!" Lattie said, on the verge of tears.

"Why would you need one? I didn't need one to put the cookies up there. When you can reach the cookies without a trampoline or a ladder, you will be a true master."

Then Master Three Claws smiled and walked away. Lattie gritted her teeth, looked up at the shimmering box of cookies . . . and began jumping.

For the next several years, Lattie stood in the Combat Hall every morning and jumped for the cookies for hours on end. She couldn't climb the walls because they were too flat,

but she found that she could gain some height by pushing off the sides with her strong legs.

After practicing, Lattie would be exhausted. At bedtime, she could hardly keep her eyes open. But every night, Master Three Claws would go into her room and tell her a fable before she went to bed. A fable is a story with a moral or lesson at the end. Lattie's favorite one was about the Sword of Gold.

"Tell the Sword of Gold fable!" Lattie would say.

"Very well," said Master Three Claws, stroking his wrinkly face and twirling his long whiskers. "Many years ago, when I was a young monster, the terrible

Mountain Dragon attacked this temple. She didn't like that we lived on 'her' mountain and declared that she was going to burn our temple to the ground. I warned the dragon that the mountains belong to everyone and are to be shared. She didn't listen and started blowing streams of fire. I warned her one last time that she would pay dearly if she didn't fly away. She just laughed. She was an enormous dragon and thought no tiny monsters could possibly hurt her. But she knew not that we had acquired the Sword of Gold so we could protect the mountain villages. Armed with the sword, I dodged the dragon's fire and snapping jaws and plunged it into her snout. With her last ounce of strength, the dragon flew away to perish beside her Elder Dragon sisters. Now, can you tell me what was the dragon's mistake?"

"She thought she couldn't be defeated," Lattie replied.

"That's right. Always remember, real knowledge is to know the extent of one's ignorance."

Seven years after she first started jumping for the cookies, Lattie was finally able to reach them. She bounced up the sides of two walls until she was able to leap upward and grasp onto one of the mounted swords. In one swift move, she pulled the sword from its sheath and jabbed it into the wall, still hanging

168

from its handle. Then she grabbed another sword with her toe and flung it so that it stuck at a higher place on the wall. She stood on it and then bounced off the first sword like a springboard, landed on the second sword, sprang off that sword, and landed on the platform.

Lattie opened the box and took her first bite of a cookie in seven years. It was as stale as cardboard but still tasted like heaven. Millie crawled down her arm and gobbled up the rest of the cookies before Lattie could even enjoy them.

Lattie laughed to herself. "There's always someone who's hungrier than you."

"Well," said Master Three Claws with a grin, "it seems as though we have a new master at the temple."

All of the ninja monsters roared and applauded. That night at dinner, Lattie was presented with her first all-black ninja uniform and a black mask to go with it. It was the happiest moment of her life.

But later, Master Three Claws came into Lattie's room with a serious look on his face. "Master Lattie, I have taught you all I can. It is time for you to leave us and go to school with children your own age. Here." Master Three Claws handed her an envelope. "This is your letter of acceptance into Scary School."

"No!" said Lattie. "I don't want to go! This is my home. I am a ninja. Not a schoolgirl."

"My dear, a flower is happiest when it is among a garden of other flowers."

Lattie ran out of her room and dove into her crawl space, shouting, "I'm not going, no matter what you say!" She couldn't bear the idea of leaving. Master Three Claws was like a father to her, and she knew she would be homesick without him there. She had no clue how to relate to other children. Especially human ones. She curled up with Millie, sobbing her eyes out, thinking: Some ninja master I am.

Suddenly, a horrific noise shook the entire temple. Lattie heard screaming and roaring, crackling and smashing. She peered out of the floorboard, where Master Three Claws was staring her right in the face.

"You stay there!" he commanded as he pulled the kitchen cabinet off the wall and put it over the floorboard so she couldn't get out even if she wanted to.

Above her, she could hear a tremendous battle raging. She had no idea what would be dumb enough to attack a ninja temple. Then she heard a terrifying voice say, "Where is the sword that slew my sister? Where is the Sword of Gold?"

It was one of the other Elder Dragons!

Lattie began punching through the floorboard to try to get out. She had to help.

There was more fighting, more screaming. She felt chilly gusts of wind blowing through the cracks.

Then she heard her master's voice: "Do not hurt them!"

"Only you possess the wise wizard's full prophecy," replied the dragon. "Give it to me and I may spare your life."

"Never!" replied Three Claws.

"So be it. Then you shall be my prisoner until you decide otherwise."

Finally, Lattie's hand broke through the board, but now the commotion had ceased and there was only an eerie silence.

She leaped out of the floor and saw that the dragon was no longer there. All the monster students were frozen in ice, their eyes lifeless. She ran to the Combat Hall and saw the Sword of Gold was missing from its glass casing.

Lattie searched desperately for Master Three Claws but could not find him anywhere. She prayed he wasn't eaten. She ran out onto the mountain ledge and saw the terrible Ice Dragon flying toward the horizon in the ghostly moonlight. In one talon—the Sword of Gold. In its other talon—the limp body of her master.

Sitting on her bed in shock, Lattie reached for the envelope her master had tried to give her just a half hour before. She opened it and found the acceptance certificate to Scary School, along with addresses of former temple pupils who would take her in. Also inside the envelope was an old piece of parchment paper. Written on it was the only copy of Marlin's original prophecy:

A dragon slayer shall emerge,
Of human heart and human mind,
To fight the dragon made of ice
And save all monsterkind.

Lattie had no idea where the Ice Dragon was hiding her master, but she figured the best place to find answers would be at school.

So now you know why Lattie began growling upon hearing that the Ice Dragon was coming. However, it was not a growl of fear, but of utmost anticipation.

17
Severed Head of the Class

The third day of class, the students walked down Corridor Three. There didn't seem to be anything scary about it at all, which made the students more scared of this corridor than all the others combined.

When the students got to the middle of the hallway, it filled up with a thick mist. Nobody could see an inch in front of their faces. Then two glowing red eyes appeared in the mist. There was a loud clopping sound combined with shrieking laughter as the glowing red eyes approached them.

"Run!" shouted Jason.

Everyone began running forward as fast as they could, until they crashed through their classroom doorway and fell on top of one another.

The glowing red eyes continued toward them, and then the impression of a man riding on a big black horse came into focus. The horse leaped over the pile of kids and galloped around the classroom. The rider was wearing a cape and a riding suit that looked centuries old.

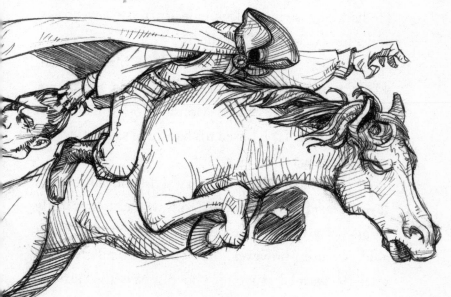

"Good morning, class," said the rider. "I see we have new victims—I mean, students. My name is Mr. Dullahan. Come in and take your seats."

That's when the kids noticed that the voice was not coming from the usual place. It was coming from a detached head being held in the teacher's arms. On top of his neck, there was *nothing*.

"You may know me best by my other name . . . the Headless Horseman!"

The headless teacher tied his black horse to a hitch next to the teacher's desk. Then he turned to the students, holding his severed head high over his neck. His eyes peered down at the students disapprovingly. He had long, stringy black hair, thick dark eyebrows, and a long scar across his cheek.

"Tell me," said the severed head of Mr. Dullahan, which spoke with a noticeable Irish lilt, "why are you not reading chapter five of your Monster Compendiums?"

Tommy the Troll raised his hand and said, "Because we just got here."

Mr. Dullahan became angry. His body threw his severed head at Tommy the Troll, who caught it softly in his hefty hands. The head said, "Normally I don't abide excuses; however, that was a particularly good one. Be warned: anyone who disobeys the headless horseman will soon find themselves just as headless!"

Mr. Dullahan pulled out a wooden ax with a long jagged blade. He swung it back and forth. The students in the front row had to duck out of the way.

"Throw me back!"

Tommy threw the head back to its body.

"In my class, as in life, the most important thing is never to lose one's head! Ha-ha! Now, everyone take out your monster compendiums and turn to chapter five."

In a unified movement of remarkable swiftness, all of the Scream Academy students pulled out their compendiums and flipped to chapter five. Unfortunately, the Scary School students were not given compendiums.

Enraged, Mr. Dullahan threw his head toward Fred. Fred was not expecting this, and the head clonked him right on the noggin. He fell backward onto the floor. Mr. Dullahan's head was resting on his chest, sneering.

Fred exclaimed, "Ew! Gross!" He picked

up the head and tossed it behind him.

As the Scary School hockey goalie, Jason had lightning-quick reflexes and caught the head before it landed on his desk.

"I'm glad someone was paying attention," said Mr. Dullahan. "Tell me, boy. Where is your Monster Compendium?"

Jason replied, "The six of us are exchange students from Scary School. Nobody gave us our books yet."

"I see. Normally I don't abide excuses. But *that* . . . is a remarkably good one. Turn me to the girl in front of you."

Jason turned the head around to face Wendy Crumkin.

"You! Go to the cabinet and get the spare Monster Compendiums for your friends, on the double!"

Wendy nodded and ran to the cabinet.

"Turn me back around for heaven's sake!"

Jason turned the head so it faced him.

"One last thing. Hiding your face is against the rules in my class. A mistake worthy of a beheading. Why are you wearing that hockey mask?

"Because," explained Jason, "everyone says I'm better-looking with the mask on."

"I see. As I said before, I don't abide excuses in my

class, but *that* . . . is the best excuse I've ever heard. You may keep your masked head attached to your body."

Wendy gave Monster Compendiums to each of her classmates.

"Throw me back!" the head demanded.

Jason tossed the head casually over his shoulder, and Lattie caught it.

"I didn't mean back*ward*," grumbled Mr. Dullahan. "I meant back to my body!"

Lattie hurled the head back at the body, but due to her stupendous ninja strength from years of throwing ninja stars, the head flew back to him much harder than he was expecting. Mr. Dullahan's head slipped through his hands and hit him in the gut, knocking the wind out of his body. His head fell on the ground, and the blunt end of the ax conked it as it rolled across the floor.

Everyone was expecting Mr. Dullahan to be furious and go on a head-chopping spree, but instead, his cranium laughed with delight while rolling on the floor. "My oh my! When it comes to you Scary School kids, it looks like I'm in way over my head!"

Everyone laughed, but the laughter ceased instantly when Mr. Dullahan held up his head and spoke: "Everyone open your Monster Compendiums to chapter five. Perhaps one of our visitors would do us the honor of reading the first page?"

Wendy Crumkin's hand shot up.

"Go ahead."

Wendy confidently stated, "Chapter five. Elder Dragons. The Elder Drag—"

But before Wendy could finish, a swirling dark cloud rose from the pages of her book. The cloud quickly formed into a mini-tornado that started sucking out all the words on the page. Then the pages were torn out of the binding and sucked into the funnel.

"Hey!" said Wendy. "Don't eat my book!" She tried to reach into the cloud to pull the pages back out, but vicious jaws snapped at her hand as if a pack of rabid dogs were inside the twister.

Within seconds, her entire book had disappeared inside the funnel, and all that remained were a few tiny shreds of paper floating above her desk.

The class was staring agape. Nobody had ever seen anything like that before.

"How strange," said Mr. Dullahan. "It seems your book had a curse placed upon it. Some sort of storm curse, maybe?" Mr. Dullahan turned his head to Charles and said, "You read!"

"Yes, sir," said Charles.

Charles began reading from the same chapter, but

as he spoke, the same tornado rose from the page and gobbled up his book.

"Egads!" shouted Mr. Dullahan. "Is it possible that two books have been cursed? There's only one way to find out. Everyone read at the same time. Go!"

The whole class started reading chapter 5, "Elder Dragons," together. But as soon as they spoke, the tornadoes rose out of each student's book.

The twisters sent each student's book flying into the air toward the center of the room. The twister was growing larger, vicious teeth were heard snapping from within, and papers were flying all over the room.

Mr. Dullahan's horse was so spooked that she started bucking up and down.

All of the desks and chairs in the classroom lifted into the air, along with the students sitting in them. The twister had grown to the ceiling and was swooshing about the room, sending backpacks, pens, pencils, and papers flying into the air. Wendy's glasses even flew right off her nose!

The trolls tried to tackle the twister but got sliced up with paper cuts. The witch girls tried to fly on their brooms, but it was too windy to have any control, and they crashed into the walls. The rest of the students clung tightly to their chairs, and they spun around the

room faster and
faster like a merry-go-
round of certain doom. Nobody could stop it.

Meanwhile, far away on the pristine beach in the Bahamas, Marlin the Fizard was having a relaxing swim in the warm tropical waters and enjoying scaring away all the tourists who thought his dorsal fin was a shark fin. It wasn't long before he had the whole beach to himself.

Then he noticed something on the shore. Beside his beach blanket, the crystal ball he brought along was glowing. He flipped out of the water, dried himself off, and gazed into its murky depths. Inside, he saw the tornado whipping

around the classroom.

Marlin had only told Charles the crystal ball was a fake so he wouldn't look into it and see his own future. *That* could cause a terrible timequake that would tear apart the fabric of the universe. At least, that's what the guy at the swap meet told Marlin when he sold him the crystal ball for twenty bucks.

"Strange," Marlin said to himself. The future always happens much faster than I remember it. His vacation having come to an abrupt end, he dove back into the water, heading toward the icy Arctic waters of Scream Academy.

Back in the classroom, as soon as all the textbooks had been swallowed, the tornado vanished just as quickly as it had arisen. Everyone's desks and chairs came crashing down to the ground in a totally different part of the classroom from where they started.

"What was that?" asked Wendy, placing her glasses back on her nose.

"Those," said Mr. Dullahan, "were bookeaters. They are the nastiest, most dangerous creatures in all the land. They feast on knowledge. They crave it like a zombie craves brains. And that's just one pack of bookeaters. There could be more hidden in any book in the world. The question is, why are they so hungry for our Monster Compendiums?"

The kids looked at one another and scratched their heads. Charles and Wendy were the creature experts, and not even they had any clue.

"Uhhh . . . ," said Tommy the Troll, "maybe they don't want us to know about a monster in the book."

Everyone looked at Tommy in shock. It may have been the smartest thing a troll had ever said.

"Of course!" said Mr. Dullahan. "The bookeaters appeared only when we started reading the chapter on Elder Dragons. And they arrived in a vicious storm. So that means . . . oh no." Mr. Dullahan turned as pale as me and dropped his head on the ground.

"Ouch!" exclaimed his head. "Be careful!" Picking up his head and wiping the dust off his hair, Mr. Dullahan walked over to a red phone hanging on the wall.

"Principal Meltington," Mr. Dullahan said, speaking into the receiver. "The Ice Dragon is coming."

As soon as Mr. Dullahan said the words *Ice Dragon*, Charles felt the same sinking feeling in stomach. Was everything Marlin the Fizard said actually true? If so, was he going to die fighting the dragon? He wanted to hide in a corner so he'd never even have to see it.

Once again, the low, guttural growl of Lattie was filling the room.

18

The Cavern of Cadavers

Minutes after Mr. Dullahan's phone call to Principal Meltington, all the students were ushered up a snowy mountain into the Scream Academy assembly hall, also known as the Cavern of Cadavers.

The cavern was built inside the biggest cave at Scream Academy. The mouth of the cave was the skull of a hundred-foot sea monster with more than five hundred teeth. Each tooth was the size of a kid.

As Charles entered the Cavern of Cadavers, he

thought it was the spookiest place he had ever set foot in. It was as broad as a soccer field and made entirely of eroded limestone. Flickering torches lined the cavern walls, creating monstrous shadows. Most limestone caves have pointy stalactites hanging from the ceiling and sharp stalagmites rising from the ground. However this cavern's stalactites had formed into the shapes of claws that seemed to be reaching down from above to snatch up those who entered.

Hundreds of stalagmites covered the ground in the shape of open hands. When the Scream Academy kids sat down on the stalagmites, Charles realized that they were naturally formed chairs! Probably the creepiest chairs in existence, but they worked. The six friends found seats together and gazed toward the front of the cavern, lit by a roaring fire, where a podium stood carved from bare rock.

A blizzard of snow swept through the cave, marking the arrival of Principal Meltington. He stood at the podium and spoke quickly, since the roaring fire that lit the cave seemed to be melting his body at an alarming rate.

"Students, I shall make this brief. Seven hundred years ago there lived an evil sorceress named Mortazella, and she had a monster servant by the name of Garzok Grubshanks."

The students cheered loudly. Garzok Grubshanks was the famous monster who had founded Scream Academy. The one whose statue stood in the school's main hall.

Meltington continued, "Mortazella was cruel and would not allow Garzok to go to school, no matter how much he begged. So Garzok taught himself to read, and he secretly read all of the books in the sorceress's library. One day, Garzok escaped and ran away as far as he could, high into these Arctic mountains. Here, he built Scream Academy and began teaching monsters what he had learned, which would eventually be the key to setting us all free. As Garzok famously said, 'Education is the path to freedom.'"

The monsters in the crowd cheered even louder.

This was their favorite story. Meltington's legs had melted up to his knees. He spoke more quickly.

"But Mortazella was not so easily defeated. She created the bookeaters. They ravaged all the books and writings of the monsters in hopes that Scream Academy would have to close down. But that didn't stop the dedicated monsters. They still took classes, using only their memories, and became smarter than ever! Enraged, Mortazella and her three sorceress sisters transformed themselves into the four Elder Dragons and set forth to attack Scream Academy."

A rat-faced monster squeezed Fred's hand in fear, but Fred told him not to be afraid because this was all just a dream. The rat-faced monster got a confused look on his face and twitched his whiskers, but he actually seemed relieved.

"Garzok Grubshanks worked tirelessly until he had forged the most powerful swords ever created. The Sword of Salt, the Sword of Silver, the Sword of Gold, and the Sword of Fire. Mortazella attacked Scream Academy in the form of the Ice Dragon, and her sisters were the Mountain Dragon, the Sky Dragon, and the Sea Dragon. It was a terrible battle, but in the end, Garzok Grubshanks slew the Ice Dragon with the Sword of Fire."

The crowd burst into applause. Meltington's legs had melted up to his hips, and he was half as tall as he was before.

"Yes, and once the Ice Dragon was defeated, the other three dragons flew off to destroy the other swords, but all were defeated by the powerful monsters who wielded the swords. The dragons came back here to die, transforming into the three mountains that surround the school. In fact, the skull we just walked through is the skull of the Sea Dragon herself."

"Ewww!" the students exclaimed.

"I agree. It's quite disgusting. And now for the  bad news. Grubshanks only thought he slew the Ice Dragon. But he had actually only wounded her. The spirit of Mortazella had remained alive and swore to one day return. It seems that day has come."

The students gasped.

"Yes. The signs are clear. The bookeaters have returned and are bent on devouring all our knowledge. It can mean only one thing. Mortazella has become the Ice Dragon once again and will soon be attacking Scream Academy to destroy it for good."

The students were speechless.

"But now for the good news. Before he died, Garzok left us the Sword of Fire in case it was ever needed again. He hid the sword and announced that when the time came, the true dragon slayer would be able to find it and defeat the Ice Dragon once and for all. I am happy to announce," said Meltington with emphasis, even though he had melted up to his shoulders, "that the true dragon slayer is with us in the room today. The question is . . . which one of you is it?"

The students looked at one another. Then several trolls, ogres, werewolves, and vampires leaped from their seats proclaiming: "It's me!" "No, it's me!" "Yar, it be me!"

"Well," said Meltington, "there's only one way to find out. It's time to see who can find the Sword of Fire."

"Huh?" said the crowd.

"Yes, you will all get a chance to find the sword. Even our visitors from Scary School."

The crowd growled in anger. They didn't want any exchange students claiming all the glory of defending Scream Academy.

"All I can tell you is that the sword is hidden somewhere in Casualty Canyon."

The crowd became silent. Casualty Canyon was one of the few off-limits areas of Scream Academy. And if an area is off-limits at this place, death must be a certainty.

Meltington concluded by saying, "There is no time to waste. Find the sword and good lu-glub-glub-glub . . ." Meltington had completely melted, and his last words sounded like gurgles of water. His liquid remnants were swept into a bucket and placed into a flash freezer so he would be able to take solid form again as soon as possible.

As the students marched out of the cavern to search for the Sword of Fire, Charles Nukid hoped that the course of events wouldn't lead to Scary School getting attacked again.

He had a very bad feeling about this.

19

The Sword of Fire

Following the assembly, Mr. Dullahan led all the students out of the Cavern of Cadavers and onto a rocky path through the snowy mountains. It was blisteringly cold. Charles had no meat on his skinny bones and no warm clothes either. Luckily, Wendy had packed an extra jacket and loaned it to him. Unluckily, the jacket was bright pink and very girly. Charles looked completely ridiculous in it, and all the monsters laughed at him. Charles didn't care because not losing his arms to frostbite seemed more important.

The rocky path was very difficult for the human kids to negotiate. Mountainous areas are made for creatures like trolls and ogres with their thick skins, padded feet, and strong stone-gripping paws. Even Lattie, with her ninja agility, was having a rough go of it among the rocks that were covered in slippery ice. The Scream Academy kids were constantly stopping so that the Scary School kids could catch up, which was making them very frustrated.

"Yeesh," said Petunia, huffing. "I wish there were some bees around here that could lift me over these rocks."

Lattie responded, "Wishing is a futile practice. We get only what we work for."

Aggravated from the tough hike, Petunia snapped back, "You know something, ninja-girl? *You* could work on saying something nice once in a while!"

Lattie was taken aback. She stood still for a moment, contemplating Petunia's words.

Petunia felt bad almost immediately. After all, Lattie had stood up for her in class. It just bothered Petunia how Lattie thought it was her place to give advice all the time. Petunia was about to apologize, but Lattie had already vanished.

Eventually, the students reached a sign that said:

CASUALTY CANYON—ELEVATION 11,200 FEET. HOPE YOU HAD A GOOD LIFE.

As they approached, they heard an awful roar in the distance.

Mr. Dullahan looked up to see the Ice Dragon on the horizon. "Quickly!" he exclaimed. "We have little time!" The dragon's roar echoed off the walls of the canyon like an ominous pinball.

The floor of the canyon looked like it could be the surface of another planet. There were thousands of boulders the size of trucks dotting the landscape and piled on top of one another. Hot springs bubbled from the ground, and the steam smelled like rotting eggs, indicating they were sulfuric and deadly.

The deposit of boulders created thousands of crevices. The students fanned out and started searching within the cracks for the Sword of Fire. Jason reached into a promising one, but a snake popped its head out and hissed at him as if to say, "Stay out of my home, Hockeyface!" Fred reached into a crevice, but a scorpion popped out and snapped its pincers as if to say, "Step off! I've got poison coming out of my tail. Literally!"

There were so many holes to search it seemed like it would take weeks to search them all. With the Ice

197

Dragon undoubtedly about to attack the school at any moment, there seemed to be no hope.

Wendy Crumkin was searching the crevices nearest the canyon wall. Everyone else thought the sword would be hidden deeper in the canyon and that she was wasting her time, but Wendy believed Garzok Grubshanks would have wanted the sword to be easily found if it were needed in an emergency.

"Awwfff, we'll *never* find the sword in time," Tommy the Troll groaned.

"I found it!" Wendy Crumkin announced with excitement, pointing at a paper-thin crevice between two stacked boulders. The students gathered around on top of one another to take a look. There was definitely something shiny in there, but the crack was so small they couldn't tell if it was a sword.

"How you know that is the sword?" asked Tommy the Troll.

"Because it says right here," said Wendy, pointing to markings on the bottom boulder.

"Those just scratches."

"No, that's ancient Monsterese. Some of the best checkers strategy books are written in ancient Monsterese, so I learned the language. It says: 'Here lies the Sword of Fire. Whoever can pull the sword from under the stone is the true dragon slayer.'"

Mrs. Basilisk, the three-headed serpent language arts teacher of Scream Academy, validated Wendy's claim.

At once there was a mad rush for the sword. Tommy the Troll pushed the others aside and tried to reach in first, but his arms were way too thick to even break the mouth of the crevice. One by one, each troll faced the same dilemma. They pounded the boulder with their fists, but it didn't budge.

The ogres fared no better than the trolls. The zombie kids' arms kept breaking off inside. Ezelba tried a summoning spell, but the sword just rattled about in its resting place and didn't come out any farther.

The students from Scary School were the only ones left.

The trolls started protesting, "Humans no get to try for sword! They too weak to be dragon slayer!"

"Humans better as food than friends!" said a lumpy troll girl.

That's when Principal Meltington appeared at the cliff's edge, having returned to his snowman form. Everyone turned their attention upward.

"Hurry, young ones! I can see the dragon coming! Give them a chance or we're doomed!"

The Scary School students stepped forward. Jason and Fred reached in. They managed to get farther than any of the monsters but couldn't even touch the handle. Petunia and Wendy made it farther than Jason and Fred but could not make contact.

Finally, Lattie appeared in front of the boulder. She was secretly glad no one else had gotten the sword, for she was desperate to be the one who would slay the dragon that stole her master. She uttered a mantra to herself: "My arm is a noodle in hot soup." She waved her left arm, and it undulated just like a wet noodle, as if she had somehow managed to will her bones away. She reached into the crevice, her hand slithering between the boulders. She touched the sword handle with her fingertips but could reach no farther.

Reluctantly, she pulled her arm out without the sword. She stomped her foot on the ground, furious that she couldn't get it. And judging by the sounds of the crowd's groans, they were certain she was the last hope.

The only one left was Charles Nukid. All eyes were fixed on him.

"No," he said. "I don't want to. I don't want to fight the Ice Dragon!" Panic was coursing through his veins. As soon as he saw the crevice, he knew that his toothpick arms were the only ones skinny enough to reach the sword. He couldn't stop thinking about Marlin's prophecy: That he would end up no more than a statue. A story. A fizard's memory. "I don't want to do it! I don't want to—"

Lattie reached back and smacked him across the face. Not in a mean way. Just hard enough to snap him out of it. She considered giving him some kind of sage advice to inspire him to action, but then she remembered what Petunia had told her just moments ago. It's rude to give unwelcome advice. So instead she said to Charles, "If you don't want to, then don't. I'll protect you."

Charles was speechless. Before him he saw a true friend who would protect him whether he was brave or cowardly. At that moment, he realized he couldn't live with himself if he did not at least try to protect her in return. For the Ice Dragon would leave none alive.

Charles threw off Wendy's pink jacket and reached into the crevice. His right arm slipped in easily. He grasped the handle and pulled out the sword in one swift motion.

The crowd gasped in awe.

The sword was bigger than he was, but it felt as

light as a feather. The handle was red as ruby and the blade was jagged as flames.

The students fell to their knees, but Tommy the Troll did not kneel. He snarled and stomped toward Charles.

"Impossible!" Tommy growled. "Garzok Grubshanks was monster! Only monster can wield his sword!"

Tommy snatched the sword from Charles, but it felt as heavy as the boulder it had rested on. Try as he might, he couldn't even lift it an inch off the ground. But then Charles grasped the sword and held it high over his head, as if it were no more than a paintbrush.

Tommy backed away in awe and took his place kneeling among the others, proclaiming, "He is the dragon slayer. I am with you, Noodle-neck."

"My name is Charles Nukid," Charles said. "I am the dragon slayer. I want everyone to know that—"

"No time for speeches!" Principal Meltington hollered from the cliff. "The dragon is here!"

The students hustled as fast as they could toward the school, Charles leading the way with the sword pointed in front of him like a spear, and Meltington flying beside him as an angry blizzard.

They arrived at the wolf's mouth and searched the skies for the dragon. It was nowhere in sight.

"I thought you said the dragon was here."

"It . . . it was," Meltington stammered. "I swear it was in the sky a moment ago."

Suddenly, the Sword of Fire began shaking in Charles's hand. It felt like an unseen force was pulling it. The sword shot out of his hand and flew through the crowd of students. They had to dive out of the way to avoid getting sliced in half!

The sword ended up in the hand of a tall, raven-haired sorceress who had appeared in a burst of smoke. She wore a long black dress, a black cape, and a metallic headdress that looked like an oversized crown.

"It is I! The great Mortazella!" she proclaimed, holding up the Sword of Fire and shooting bolts of lightning from her wand. "I've been waiting hundreds of years for a dragon slayer to pull the Sword of Fire from the stone. Now that the sword is mine, there is nothing that can stop me from destroying this unspeakable school!"

Principal Meltington approached her, steaming with anger. "Can't you see that you are wrong about monsters not being free to learn? Just look at this glorious school and the brilliant monsters it produces."

Tommy the Troll chose the worst moment possible to release a loud *belch*.

"This school is a disgrace!" declared Mortazella. She pointed her wand and shot a lightning bolt at Meltington. Electricity surged through his snowman body, and he instantly evaporated into steam.

The students gasped. Their brave principal would not be able to return as himself until the next snowfall. With one spell, it was as if Mortazella had ripped the hearts out of all the students and teachers.

Mortazella laughed. "And now to end Scream Academy once and for all!"

The sorceress placed the sword in her belt and wrapped herself in smoke rings. From the smoke emerged a tall and terrible dragon. It continued growing until it was more than five hundred feet tall, towering over the top spires of Scream Academy itself.

Mortazella had transformed into the infamous Ice Dragon, shimmering white with crystal scales, silver wings, and icicle spikes on her tail. In a display of fearsome power, she roared over the crowd, and her icy breath stung like a thousand needles.

She turned to one of the spires and blasted a stream of snow from her dragon mouth, which sent the castle's stones crashing to the ground. The fearsome wolf-head entrance came to life, barking and snarling at the dragon. The dragon wasn't scared one bit and smashed the bottom jaw of the wolf's head with one mighty whip of her spiked tail.

In awe of her power, Tommy the Troll turned to his friends and said, "Welp, this was fun while it lasted. I guess it's time for us trolls to head back to our caves."

The trolls nodded in agreement and started to retreat, but then Petunia ran in front of the exit gates and shouted, "Now is not the time to give up! This is *your* school. You have a right to your education. Nobody can take that away from you."

"Look," said Tommy. "This school's great and all, but not worth dying for."

Petunia gritted her teeth. She couldn't stand to see people bullied like she had so often been. If she had listened to those who said there's no place for a purple girl, she would never have found Scary School. But, she also realized, maybe it wasn't her place to tell these kids what was worth fighting and possibly dying for.

The trolls, ogres, vampires, witches, werewolves, zombies, and monsters pushed past her as they exited through the gates, defeated and downtrodden, unable to bear watching their school being destroyed behind them.

Jason saw Hubert in the crowd and shouted, "Come on, Hubert! Not *you*!"

Hubert looked like he wanted to stay, but his snowkid friends pushed him forward. He lowered his head and followed them through the gate.

The Ice Dragon laughed. "Ha-ha! No one can stop me this time. And after I'm finished turning Scream Academy into rubble, my next stop will be Scary School!"

The Scary School kids gasped. If they let the Ice

Dragon win, all of their friends at Scary School would face the wrath of the Ice Dragon without any warning. They looked at one another, knowing that as brave students of Scary School, there was no way they were going to let the Ice Dragon succeed without at least trying to stop her.

Once again, it was all up to them. But this time, they had no plan whatsoever.

20

Just Winging It

As the dragon continued smashing the wolf's head to pieces with her tail and blowing jets of snow at Scream Academy's bridges and towers, the six Scary School students huddled together.

Fred said, "Looks like we're the only ones left to stop the dragon. What an awesome dream, right, guys?" No one dared tell him it wasn't a dream so he wouldn't chicken out. They needed their class hero now more than ever.

Jason said, "We must get the Sword of Fire back. That's the one thing that can stop the Ice Dragon."

"But how?" said Petunia. "The sword is still in the

belt around its neck. That's like, a thousand feet high."

"I have an idea," said Wendy. She reached into her backpack and pulled out a jar of bright green liquid.

"Is that dragonfly potion?" asked Charles.

"Yep. I made some this morning. It was going to be a present for my brother."

"But I thought you weren't paying attention when Ms. Coven taught us how to make it," said Fred.

"Duh! Of course I was paying attention. I just wasn't going to admit it in front of all those hungry monsters."

"Yes! Let's do this!" exclaimed Jason.

"I'm in!" said Fred.

"Me too," said Petunia.

"And me," said Charles.

Lattie simply nodded, her eyes burning with anticipation.

Wendy applied the potion to everyone's backs and then put some on herself. Dragonfly wings sprouted from their shoulder blades and they each took flight, heading in a straight line toward the dragon's head.

Lattie led the team. She turned to them and said, "Flank the dragon's head to distract her while Charles and I get the sword."

The team nodded in agreement.

Lattie grabbed Charles and pulled him by her side as she flew toward the dragon's neck.

Jason pulled out his hockey stick and flew to the dragon's left side. Fred pulled out his silver hammer and flew to her right. Petunia took perhaps the bravest course of all. She flew directly in front of the dragon's face, knowing her purple coloring would be a distraction.

Petunia hovered in position, rising in front of the dragon's nose. She thought, So this is what it feels like to be one of the bugs that buzz around my hair.

The dragon roared, seeing Petunia floating in front of her face. "Have you gone mad, purple girl?"

"*This* is madness," said Petunia. "Stop this destruction, or else!"

The dragon laughed. "Or else what?" she said, spewing a stream of snowy ice toward Petunia. She dodged it with the agility of one of her bumblebee friends. Her time spent observing their flight technique was unexpectedly paying off!

The distraction had worked brilliantly. The dragon was so busy firing snow blasts at Petunia, she had no idea Lattie and Charles had landed on her back and were inching their way toward the belt.

When Petunia looked to be in trouble, Jason and

Fred buzzed past to draw the dragon's attention. The entire time, Wendy was hovering nearby, punching numbers on her calculator. She called out to her friends, "According to my calculations, she can shoot an ice blast only every eight point six seconds. Plan your strikes accordingly!"

So the friends focused their taunting in short, eight-second bursts, then took cover as the dragon fired a wild snow blast. Then they dove back in.

Meanwhile, Lattie and Charles had made it to the belt, but the dragon was thrashing so wildly they were using all their strength just to hang on.

Millie the Millipede crawled out from Lattie's sleeve, slinked onto the belt, and loosened the sword from its encasement.

Lattie reached out and pulled on the sword, but alas, the sword felt as heavy as a house in her hands, and it slipped through her grip, plummeting toward the ground.

Charles leaped off the dragon's back and flew after the sword, but in the midst of his flight, the dragonfly spell wore off, and Charles's situation turned from a downward flight to a hopeless free fall in an instant.

Well, here I am plummeting toward certain death again, thought Charles.

One by one, the dragonfly wings on each of the students disintegrated, leaving Lattie stuck to the dragon's back, Jason and Fred clutching tightly to the dragon's ears, and Petunia holding on for dear life to the dragon's snout. Wendy was already back on the ground, trying to come up with a new plan.

The Sword of Fire landed blade-down in the snow, but it didn't matter because when Charles landed, he was going to end up a mangled mess.

He closed his eyes, sure this had to be the end.

21

A Good Day to Die

Charles suddenly felt himself in the arms of something furry. He slowly opened his eyes, not sure if he was still alive. A blue furry face with long banana teeth and a big bushy unibrow was looking at him.

"Don't worry. I got you," said Rory.

Beneath the blue monster was one of the polter-bears, and sitting behind the blue monster . . . was Penny Possum!

"Penny!" exclaimed Charles. "What are you doing here?"

Penny smiled, then pointed to her left. In a flash of

light, two polter-bears entered through portals. On the back of the first one was Johnny the Sasquatch and Ramon the Zombie, and on the second was Peter the Wolf, Cy Clops, and Hubert the Snowkid.

"Hey, Nukid," said Johnny. "Hubert told us you needed some help, so we all volunteered."

"Snowdy!" said Hubert. "I wasn't gonna let you face the Ice Dragon all alone. I just had to make the others think that so I could sneak off and grab the polter-bears. I'm with you guys all the way."

The polter-bears disappeared and all seven fell into the snow.

"What's the problem?" said Ramon. "Is there a troll that wants to smush you? We'll take care of him!"

"Um . . . it's a little bit bigger than a troll," said Charles. He pointed to the Ice Dragon, which was in the middle of spewing another ice blast at a Scream Academy tower, sending it tumbling to the ground.

His friends' eyes became as big as grapefruits, then they glared at Charles.

"Seriously, Nukid, what is it with you?" said Peter the Wolf. "Every time you go someplace it ends up getting attacked by something unbelievably horrifying!"

Charles could only shrug his shoulders as the blue monster set him down in the snow.

"My name is Rory," said Rory. "I not afraid to help you. What the plan?"

At that moment, Lattie, Jason, Fred, and Petunia were still hanging on to the dragon's head for dear life. She roared, "Foolish humans are nothing more than fleas!" She thrashed and whipped her body to shake them off but only succeeded in tiring herself out.

Lattie took the opportunity and whistled to the others to follow her. She let go and slid down the dragon's tail like a slide—the longest, most slippery slide *ever*! Jason, Fred, and Petunia ran across the dragon's head, jumped on to her back, and slid down after Lattie.

"Whoooa!" they shouted, zipping down the neck, speeding down the spine, and skidding down the tail. The tip was curled upward. They slipped between the spikes and were sent airborne, crashing into the snow next to their friends.

The dragon turned her attention to them. Her eyes glowed a frightening white with rage. "Where is the Sword of Fire?" the dragon bellowed.

The sword was still planted in the snow, just a few feet in front of Charles. He stepped toward the sword, lifted it out of the powder, and as he held it aloft, the blade ignited in flames. The friends' jaws dropped in unison.

218

The dragon laughed at Charles. "Ha-ha-ha! You are no dragon slayer. Look at you! It's a miracle you can even hold up the sword. But I am not without a heart. I will give you this one chance. You and your friends must turn away and leave, and I will spare your lives. Otherwise, you will not survive this day."

Charles turned to his friends.

"I don't think we're going to get a better deal than that," said Ramon.

"Yeah, I say we take it," said Peter. "We gave it our best shot. It's not even our school."

Charles retorted, "No! The dragon said after this will be Scary School, and then the rest of the schools—Bloodington, Wolfsbane, Zombie Tech. They all could be gone if we don't make a stand right now."

"It's your call, dude," said Fred. "You're the dragon slayer."

"We're behind you no matter what," added Jason.

Charles was still unsure. He knew Marlin's prophecy foretold certain death if he faced the dragon. Could he really walk straight into it? Or was this the moment of truth when he could make a different choice and change the future?

Petunia and Lattie each put an arm on his shoulders. Petunia said, "You are the dragon slayer, Charles.

Who else could survive Dr. Dragonbreath's class?"

Lattie added, "Fear is the dragon within. Conquer your dragon."

But it was Penny's words that affected him the most. "(Silence)," said Penny, and he knew exactly what he had to do.

Charles stepped forward, looked the dragon straight in the eye, held up the fiery sword and proclaimed, "We are not afraid of you, Ice Dragon! If we must die to stop you, then today is a good day to die! Chaaarge!"

With the fiery sword shining like a beacon before them, the brave students charged toward the Ice

Dragon. The dragon reared back, took in a deep breath, and blew an avalanche of snow at the students—enough to bury them alive in a mountain of snow, never to be seen again.

But the Sword of Fire had a different plan. The flames began dancing on the blade, and before the avalanche could hit, the flames leaped into the air and formed a wall of fire around the students. The wall of fire was so hot that when the snow hit it, it sizzled and transformed into harmless steam.

Oh my goodness, thought Charles. If I had dropped the sword and run away, that snow blast would have buried us alive!

The Ice Dragon grew alarmed. Covered by the impenetrable wall of fire, the students rushed under the dragon's belly as Charles climbed onto the dragon's tail and exclaimed, "Rule breakers must be punished, fiend!"

The dragon ignored the other students and focused her attention on Charles. She uncoiled her long neck toward her tail and started snapping at him, but he swung wildly with the sword and the dragon recoiled, afraid of the sword grazing her face. So the dragon whipped her tail, sending Charles flying through the air and the sword flying out of his hands.

Charles screamed, "Aaaagh!" as he soared through the air, desperately reaching for the sword, but it landed in the snow a hundred feet away from him, extinguishing its flames.

Charles got up and tried to run to the sword, but he immediately fell down in agony. His ankle was badly sprained. He couldn't put an ounce of weight on it.

Charles was alone on the ground, holding on to his

ankle, trying to rub the pain away. The Ice Dragon was laughing again, moving closer toward him.

The other Scary School students were trying to distract her, but the Ice Dragon focused her attention on Charles and blew a wall of ice around him. He was trapped. His friends couldn't break through to reach him.

"Any last words?" asked the Ice Dragon in the sorceress's cold voice, licking her chops in anticipation of a Charles Nukid meal.

Charles tried to think of something memorable to say, but nothing came to mind. Then the answer fell from the sky. A wrapped box flew over the wall and landed in his lap.

"What's this?" Charles said aloud.

"Your last words are 'what's this'? Okay. It's your gravestone." As the dragon opened her mouth, Charles felt her icy breath all over his body. He patted his hair and straightened his polka-dot tie, ready to meet his fate.

22

The Last Meal

When Charles opened his eyes a moment later, he was absolutely shocked that he had not been eaten.

The Ice Dragon had halted mid-bite and was looking at him strangely.

"What's that in your hand?" the dragon asked.

"It . . . it looks like a present," Charles answered, a little confused.

"From who?"

Charles saw a note on the

box that said, *From Penny.* "Oh! It's from my friend!"

"I'm not without a heart," said the dragon. "You may open your present before I eat you."

Charles carefully unwrapped the paper. It was a box of Possum's Hot Peppers. He lifted the lid, and inside were dozens of bright orange peppers. The death peppers.

Great, thought Charles. Some last meal.

"Well? What is it?" asked the dragon.

That's when Charles had the idea of a lifetime. However, it would require him to break a rule and tell a fib. Charles was mortally afraid of breaking a rule.

But he pushed aside his fear, figuring it was his only hope.

"Umm . . . it's a box of chocolates," Charles said to the dragon.

"Chocolates! My favorite!" said the smiling dragon. "Tell you what, if you feed me the chocolates, I won't chew you for too long."

"It's a deal," said Charles.

The dragon opened her mouth wide and grinned in chocolaty anticipation.

Charles chucked the entire box of orange peppers into the dragon's mouth. In her excitement, the dragon instantly chewed and swallowed all the peppers.

The dragon's expression slowly changed from joy to horror as steam blew out of her ears.

"Those weren't chocolates!" the dragon choked.

"Oops," said Charles, showing her the box of hot peppers with Mr. Possum's photo on it.

The dragon roared and started running around. She tried to blow a stream of ice from her mouth, but all that came out was a stream of fire. The Ice Dragon plunged her face into the snow to extinguish the heat, but the ice just turned to water and spread the heat all over her insides.

Now the dragon was in real agony. As the peppery

heat coursed through her veins, all of the ice that formed the dragon's scales started melting. Fuming with anger, the dragon shot a desperate blast of fire at Charles, but Charles ducked out of the way. The fire melted the ice wall that trapped him!

With the ice wall down, Lattie pulled Charles out of the way, and they joined Petunia, Jason, Fred, and Wendy, who had taken cover behind a large rock.

The dragon was thrashing about, causing her icy body to melt all the more quickly. Then the sorceress's magic wand, which the dragon had been grasping in her claws, flew through the air and landed in the hand of Petunia.

"Please," begged the dragon, "Shout 'milkus eruptus.' It will shoot a jet of milk into my mouth."

Petunia thought about it. Well, even though she's evil, I guess it's the right thing to do.

Petunia raised the wand and shouted, "Milkus—"

But before she could complete the spell, the wand was snatched out her hand. The students turned. Only Charles recognized who had snatched the wand.

It was Marlin the Fizard.

"Little girl," said Marlin, "there are rare occasions when doing the right thing is not the right thing. This is one of them. Charles, I hope you remember the dragon's weak spot."

Charles nodded. He pulled the Sword of Fire from the snow and limped over to the shrinking dragon. He held the sword up toward the dragon's nose and barely touched it. Fire exploded from within the dragon's gut, melting the rest of the ice, and leaving only the sorceress Mortazella standing, defeated and without her wand.

Marlin approached Mortazella, still gripping her wand.

"Marlin!" exclaimed Mortazella. "How did you escape the ice?"

Marlin pointed with his sword nose. "This boy

freed me from your spell."

"He must be a very powerful wizard," said Mortazella.

"No," said Marlin. "He's just a brave kid with some good friends."

The twelve students smiled at one another.

"Please," she said. "I'll give anything for a glass of milk."

"I know just what will cool you off," said Marlin.

"No! Wait!" shouted Lattie. "She has to tell me where my master is!"

But it was too late. Marlin had shot an ice blast from the wand, and in an instant, Mortazella was frozen in a block of ice. "That ought to keep you cool for another few hundred years, sorceress. In fact, I know it will! I've seen you there!"

Realizing the Ice Dragon was beaten, the students of Scream Academy stormed back through the gates. They rushed toward the Scary School students as fast as they could.

The trolls lifted Charles up on their shoulders, chanting, "Noodle-neck! Noodle-neck!" The ogres lifted Lattie, the yetis lifted Jason and Fred, and the witch girls gave Wendy a broom to fly on. Rory released a bloodcurdling roar that knocked everyone over and surprised even himself.

Charles jumped down and gave Marlin a hug. "I guess you were wrong about my future," Charles said to him.

"What are you talking about?" said Marlin, confused. "You're Charles Nukid, the famous dragon slayer. Two hundred years from now, your statue still stands, commemorating your remarkable victory over the Ice Dragon."

Of course, thought Charles. That's the future that Marlin remembers now! I really did change it!

When Charles thought back to that terrible day when his picnic with Penny had ended in disaster, he couldn't help but laugh. If it hadn't been for everything going so badly, Penny might never have brought the hot peppers to Scream Academy and come to his rescue, and Charles would not have survived his battle with the Ice Dragon.

Charles had learned a very important life lesson, and he didn't even have to die in the process. Sometimes bad things happen, but it's not until later that you realize it was all for the best.

Lattie appeared in front of Charles.

"Thanks for saving me," he said, giving her a respectful bow. Lattie bowed back to Charles, but then he noticed that tears were dripping from her mask.

"What's wrong?" he asked.

"The Ice Dragon stole my master. Now I fear I'll never be able to find him."

Overhearing the conversation, Marlin popped his swordfish head in between, nearly spearing them both.

"Excuse me," said Marlin. "Did you say the Ice Dragon took your master? Well, now that we have her wand, it shouldn't be much trouble to bring him back. Tell me, what's his name?"

"Master Three Claws."

Marlin waved the wand and chanted, "Zalakazam zalakazaws! Bring me Master Three Claws!"

Master Three Claws appeared in a puff of smoke right in front of them. He opened his eyes as if waking from a deep sleep and immediately recognized Lattie.

"Master Lattie? Where am I?" murmured Three Claws.

"Where you are matters far less than whose heart you are in," Lattie replied. Then she jumped into his arms and hugged him harder than she ever had before.

The six exchange students from Scary School couldn't have had a better time at Scream Academy the rest of the week. Actually, Jason got bruised pretty badly from playing monster hockey with Hubert, but he figured that all the bumps and scrapes just added to his good looks.

Each Scary School student was considered a Scream Academy hero, and the monster students fought over who got to be better friends with them. Nobody ever complained about humans at the school again.

When it was time to leave, the Scary School kids were given a big going-away party in Garzok Hall. Witches flew around on brooms, dropping candy for the kids to catch in their mouths.

Wendy won a school-wide game of pin-the-tail-on-the-dragon. Her dragonfly potion helped out a lot, though the dragon student who got his tail pinned was a little upset.

Petunia painted the walls with purple petunias so that the monsters could see what flowers looked like. Fred danced with all the cute zombie girls and still couldn't believe his dreams kept getting more and more fantastic.

Lattie took down a two-ton troll with ease during the championship sumo-wrestling match. Dumbfounded, Silence the Yeti asked, "How did you beat someone who weighs so much more than you?"

Lattie replied, "The boulder weighs more than the rock, but which would you rather have in your hand during a fight?"

Charles rode into the party on the back of Mr. Dullahan's horse, holding his teacher's head high in the air. Mr. Dullahan exclaimed, "Good-bye, students of Scary School! We are all very sad that you're 'heading off!' Ha-ha-ha-ha!"

The event culminated in Principal Meltington unveiling a brand-new statue next to the one of the great Garzok Grubshanks. It was a sculpture of Charles Nukid, made out of gleaming marble. It looked remarkably like him, with the same gray shorts, white dress shirt, and polka-dot tie, except, of course, it was thirty feet tall. He was immortalized in a heroic pose, pointing the Sword of Fire skyward with a ferocious look on his face.

The inscription read: CHARLES "NOODLE-NECK" NUKID— SLAYER OF THE TERRIBLE ICE DRAGON. WIELDER OF THE SWORD OF FIRE. FRIEND TO ALL MONSTERS.

Charles loved it, except for that "Noodle-neck" part. But what's set in stone is set in stone.

Suddenly, there was a green flash of light from outside. Charles ran back through the wolf's mouth and saw Penny standing in the snow, looking upward.

In the sky was the aurora borealis, also known as the northern lights. Brilliant waves of green, pink, and blue light flashed in the sky—an effect that only

happens near the North Pole when charged energy particles collide with the atmosphere. It looked like a rainbow river was rolling across the stars.

Both thought it was the most beautiful sight they had ever seen. Penny took Charles's hand in hers, and they gazed at the sky for what seemed like hours, but may have only been minutes.

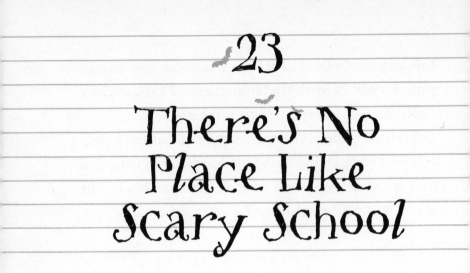

23

There's No Place Like Scary School

Every school in the Scary community had soon heard about how the Scary School students had not only survived but had also saved Scream Academy from destruction. From Bloodington to Witchbrook to Wolfsbane to Zombie Tech School for the Mostly Dead, every school was clamoring to be the next one to host Scary School exchange students.

When the students arrived back at Scary School,

they were greeted with a spectacular parade. The third and fourth graders had built a gigantic float of the Ice Dragon. It traveled down the street as the Scary School band marched beneath it, playing the Scary School song, which I'm sure you've heard if you've visited the Scary School website.

After the float, the six exchange students made their entrance. Jason and Fred were riding atop Ms. T the T. rex, waving to the adoring crowd. Wendy and Petunia followed behind them on the back of the nine-headed monitor lizard, Ms. Hydra.

"Yay! Go Petunia!" shouted Frank, which is pronounced "Rachel."

A bat appeared next to the two girls and transformed into Wendy's friend, Count Checkula Jr. He rode next to Wendy on one of Ms. Hydra's necks.

"Hi, Wendy," Count Checkula Jr. said. "I transferred to Scary School because I could not stand to be away from you a moment longer."

Wendy couldn't stop giggling for days.

Finally, Charles and Lattie swooped over the crowd, riding on the back of Dr. Dragonbreath.

Dr. Dragonbreath turned to Charles and said, "I am very pleased you survived your battle with the Ice Dragon. If any dragon is going to eat you, it's going to be me. As soon as I catch you breaking a rule, of course."

"Well," said Charles, patting Dr. Dragonbreath on his scaly back, "if any monster makes a meal of me, I hope it's you."

As a gift of gratitude, Charles was allowed to keep the Sword of Fire. He held it high as he flew over the crowd, hearing the cheers of the students and teachers. Charles had no interest in keeping the sword. He planned on sticking it under a rock somewhere as soon as he could, so as not to tempt any more trouble.

Charles searched for Penny in the crowd to see if she was cheering, but he didn't see her. Lattie was sitting behind Charles, holding on to his waist, but he wasn't feeling the same feeling as when Penny held him while flying to Monster Kingdom.

Mr. Acidbath shouted from below, "Wowzy-woozy! Show us the sword!" Charles held the sword up, but he didn't notice that the Ice Dragon float was directly above him. He punctured a hole right in the float's belly, and it deflated on top of the crowd like melted cheese.

The parade came to an end much sooner than expected.

So much for his hero status.

King Khufu pointed at him and snarled, "Death shall come upon swift wings to he who ruins a parade for a king!"

The students crawled out from under the float, and Principal Headcrusher gathered everyone around her. She raised her hands to her mouth.

"Everybody, listen!" Principal Headcrusher exclaimed. She was so loud they couldn't *not* listen if they wanted to. "We were going to have our closing ceremonies inside the world's largest toy store, and you were all going to get free toys, but I guess we'll have to make do right here."

Everyone grumbled.

"First off, let us all congratulate Wendy, Fred, Jason, Petunia, Lattie, and Charles for making us so proud by surviving Scream Academy and stopping the mighty Ice Dragon from reducing the school to rubble. And we mustn't forget the bravery of Johnny, Ramon, Peter, Cy, Rory, and Penny for helping out their friends in need. They saved not only Scream Academy but also Scary School and every school in the Scary community."

There was tepid applause. Everyone was still thinking about the toys they weren't going to get.

"I think we have all learned that bravery and the bonds of friendship can overcome even the most frightening monstrosities the world can throw at us."

The students cheered much more loudly.

"And lastly, I have a big surprise for you."

The cheering ceased immediately.

"To celebrate our glorious victory, we will be

having a dance party in Petrified Pavilion right now. I'm calling it the Dance of Destiny. That is all."

Charles saw Penny pop out of the crowd from behind Mr. Grump. He ran as fast as he could to her. When he reached her, he was so out of breath that he could barely speak.

"Penny . . . would you . . . would you . . . sorry, I just need . . . a second . . . to catch . . . okay . . . would you like to go to the—"

Charles was knocked away by the thick arm of Lebok the Troll. "Get out of here, Toothpick," growled Lebok. "Penny, you go to Dance of Destiny with Lebok."

Picking himself off the ground, Charles said, "But you pushed her into the mud!"

"Yeah. That's how trolls show they like someone. Penny goes with me."

Penny was shaking her head furiously.

"Hey, Lebok not asking. Lebok telling." Lebok lifted Penny off the ground and carried her over his shoulder. Penny was hitting his back, trying to squirm free.

Charles shouted, "Hey, Lebok!"

Lebok turned to him and snarled.

"Looks like you win again. But we should be

friends. You want a piece of candy?"

"Candy? Yes!"

Charles handed Lebok a piece of candy, and he popped it in his mouth. But of course it wasn't a piece of candy. It was a death pepper.

Lebok dropped Penny and ran in circles screaming, "Waahhhh!" before diving face-first into the town fountain. Which only made it worse.

"So," said Charles, helping Penny up. "Would you like to go to the dance with me?"

Penny said yes as softly as she could, but the force still knocked Charles backward onto his bottom. Penny lifted him up and gave him a big hug.

He had been through an awful lot to finally get that hug, but it was totally worth it.

As soon as Penny let go, Charles suddenly found himself being lifted up again and suspended hundreds of feet in the air. He looked up and saw he was clutched in the grasp of some hideous flying monster.

When he felt the furry paw and smelled the putrid smell, he knew exactly what had snatched him—a bearodactyl. The half-bear, half-pterodactyl monster that had it in for him since last semester.

"Are you going to eat me?" Charles asked the bearodactyl.

The bearodactyl answered in a voice that sounded like a parrot's. "Eat you? Not today. I'm taking you to Monster Kingdom."

"Monster Kingdom? But why?"

"Because, young human, you defeated the Monster King in battle. That means you're the new Monster King!"

"Me? The Monster King?"

As the bearodactyl soared into the distance, Charles couldn't believe he was about to be taken on yet another horrifying adventure.

Final Note from Derek the Ghost

Do you want to know what happens at the Dance of Destiny? You'll need to go to the website—www.ScarySchool.com—to find the bonus chapter and read all about it. Hopefully the bookeaters haven't gotten to it first! Search carefully, and you will find it hidden safely near one of the students of Scream Academy!

And so you've managed to survive to the end, my

loyal readers. That means you've finished reading three Scary School books. You have accomplished something rather significant. There's a word for accomplishing three major achievements in a row: a *trifecta*. And when you complete a trifecta, that automatically makes you . . . *awesome.*

In fact, whenever another kid is making fun of you or calling you names in the school yard, you will now have the right to come back with: "That's not true. I'm awesome!"

Then the other kid will say: "Oh yeah? What makes *you* awesome?"

Then you say: "I completed a trifecta. How many trifectas have *you* completed?"

They will say: "Uhhhhhh . . ."

Before they have a chance to think of one, you butt in and say: "That's right. Zero! Now why don't you go hang on the monkey bars?"

Point, set, and match. You're welcome.

Hope to see you again soon! And if you have a chance, come visit me at ScarySchool.com! Maybe we can find the bonus chapter together! Either way, may all your school days be happy and scare-free.

Your friend,

Derek the Ghost